DON'T BOTHER TO KNOCK

Out at Palmtrees Racetrack, the little man in the noisy clothes wanted Mark Preston. All Preston wanted was revenge on the bookies. He got busy with that, somebody else got busy shoving an ice-pick in the little man. People began to crawl from holes. Ice-picks came into style, back-wise. Preston preferred his back without holes. He also preferred blonde Stella Delaney, front-wise, any-wise. But that would have to wait. Rourke of Homicide was anxious to find a tenant for a cool cell with boneyard exposure.

PETER CHAMBERS

DON'T
BOTHER
TO KNOCK

Complete and Unabridged

LINFORD
Leicester

First published in Great Britain in 1966

First Linford Edition
published 2005

British Library CIP Data

Chambers, Peter, *1924*–
    Don't bother to knock.—Large print ed.—
Linford mystery library
1. Detective and mystery stories
2. Large type books
I. Title
823.9'14 [F]

ISBN 1–84395–854–6

Published by
F. A. Thorpe (Publishing)
Anstey, Leicestershire

Set by Words & Graphics Ltd.
Anstey, Leicestershire
Printed and bound in Great Britain by
T. J. International Ltd., Padstow, Cornwall

This book is printed on acid-free paper

1

The sun shone on excited faces, lighting up the hopes and worries, the concentration, despondency, ecstasy of the packed thousands. The green turf sparkled like a lush emerald as the steady drumming became louder and more insistent. The voice rumble swelled to a roar, then to a cacophonous crescendo as the brilliant colors swept by, small bundles of exotic cloth crouched on the straining, sweating horses. The sight and the atmosphere don't vary anywhere on the earth's surface, and it is an unusual man who does not feel himself caught suddenly up by the surging excitement, swept along with the brief hysterical enthusiasm as the horses tear into the finish.

Then it was done. Unity destroyed, and the crowd segregated at once into two camps. The big one, the majority wailing its misfortunes at maximum lung pressure. The little one, comprising the small percentage of bettors who had made a good forecast, heading fast to the winning windows, clutching their precious tickets.

An interesting phenomenon, that small group. I'd thought so before as I watched them pile past. They looked ordinary enough, as individuals. You wouldn't pick any of them out and say, This man is a future President, or This woman will be the new sex symbol. They just weren't that kind, they never are. And yet they all possess this thing, this indefinable ability to decide in advance which of several horses will arrive at its destination slightly ahead of its fellows. I do not possess this quality. Try as I might, I know it will always elude me, and yet I go on trying, pushing my luck. Like today for instance. Here I was, being shoved and jostled by all these unpresidential candidates and unsex symbols. Standing there, at the end of the fourth race, sadly tearing up the last of a pile of ten-dollar tickets. A man should learn, I reflected. As a man gets older he should learn by example and experience. But especially by experience. A man ought to realise that if he persists in banging his head against a wall, sooner or later the head will hurt. Nothing will happen to the wall. So I reflected wisely, and while I reflected wisely, and while I reflected, cast my eyes over the runners for the fifth.

'You're Preston, no?'

Irritated at the interruption, as well as my own stupidity, I looked around for the voice. It was coming out of a short, narrow man with very small and sharp features. He wasn't an inch above five feet in height. If I'd been wearing a coat I might just have squeezed the whole of him into one pocket.

'What did you say?' I asked vaguely.

'I said you're Preston, no?' he repeated squeakily.

'I'm Preston, yes,' I contradicted. 'Goodbye.'

I turned to walk away, but he scuttled beside me dragging on my arm.

'Wait a minute, can't you? I wanta talk to you.'

I sighed and stopped. We were next to a high fence. For a minute I was tempted to pick him up and sit him on the top.

3

People would have thought he was a decoration. He wore a Hawaiian shirt, a yellow Panama hat and white yachting pants. On his feet was a leather riot of green and yellow.

'All right, big man. Tell me what to play in the fifth.'

He shook his head so sharply I was afraid the thin neck might snap.

'You got me wrong. I don't hustle information.'

'Then what are we talking about?' I demanded. 'Goodbye again.'

'Aw, be nice. Listen, I don't wanta have to get tough.'

It was a good line and he'd used it before. I looked down at the whole half-pint of him, the doggy face eager to please. Then I grinned. I couldn't help it, although I knew he'd judged my reaction in advance. He smiled nervously in return.

'All right, tough guy, what do you want?'

Bright little eyes flicked over the surrounding packs of people.

'Not here,' he insisted, 'People watching me. You gotta car?'

4

'Out in the park. Why?'

Again the bony fingers were scrabbling at my arm.

'Let's go, huh? We can talk out there.'

Firmly I disengaged the clutching hand.

'Maybe later. Right now, I have to get back some of this sugar I've been spreading on this immortal turf.'

'No,' he said definitely. 'Now.'

In the fifth there was a horse belonging to a friend of mine. The nag was Monkton Boy, and my friends had advised me privately to sell up the family estates and drop the proceeds onto the Boy's back. I had a great yearning to see back at least some of the ill-gotten profits I'd been donating so generously all afternoon. I'd had enough of the little guy.

'Get another boy,' I snapped. 'I have some racing to do. I dropped a hundred and twenty bucks today so far. The track owes me.'

He made a sound of disgust.

'Ah. I'm talking big money, big money Preston. Don't louse me up for a few

5

measly bucks. Let's go out to the car. Listen, I'm not fooling, there's guys looking for me. I might not make the fifth.'

And suddenly he wasn't a funny little rainbow man anymore. He was a badly frightened man, and I've seen enough to know.

'Cops no good?' I asked quickly.

'Not this trip.'

Loudspeakers began to blare the runners for the fifth. I looked again at the little man, and made up my mind.

'All right. Here.'

I gave him the ignition key and told him where the Chev was.

'Get over there,' I instructed. 'I'll make my bet and follow.'

'You won't be long, huh? Not long?'

His eyes were pleading.

'Five minutes,' I promised.

He bobbed his head and ducked away among the thickening crowds heading for the windows. I got into the nearest line, my mind neatly halved between the prospect of the gold-bearing Monkton Boy, and just what I was getting into with

6

my new friend. There was quite a crowd in front of me and it was almost race time when I made the window. Taking a deep breath I plunked fifty on the Boy's nose and stuffed tickets into my pocket. People were streaming to the fence now, and I was tempted to join them. But I remembered the frightened face of the little man, shrugged my shoulders and headed away instead.

Threading my way between the packed rows of cars I came at last to where I'd dropped the Chev. There was no sign of the little guy. I stared all around, hoping to see him. He couldn't very well make himself inconspicuous in that outfit. I thought of the key, and cursed. Then I tried the door handle, and it opened smoothly. The key was planted in the ignition lock where it ought to be, so the little man had been to the car. Then for some reason, he must have decided not to stay. Well, that was all right with me, I decided. Might still be in time for the race if I hurried. I removed the key and locked up again, then walked quickly back to the track. There was an almighty roar, a lot of groaning. People began to stream away from the fence. The loud-speaker was crackling steadily but I couldn't hear what was being said against the uproar. A beefy, red-faced man lumbered by.

'I missed it,' I told him. 'What happened?'

He looked at me fiercely, to see whether I was some kind of joker.

'A bum race,' he bristled. 'A real bum race. Number Six took it.'

Oh. Number Six. Monkton Boy was — wait. Monkton Boy was Number Six. Digging feverishly in my pocket I gathered the precious pasteboard and scuttled to the window. Not such a large crowd now, less of that jostling. We were a more orderly assembly, people of calm assurance. The kind of people who don't have to rush around proving anything, because they know they are winners. The cool green bills settled comfortably into my hand, and now I had two hundred and fifty dollars. For a brief moment I thought about the next race, but I was beginning to feel concerned about my missing rainbow friend. It wouldn't hurt me just to take a look around for the guy. After all, he had said some people were after him.

In the parking lot there was more activity now. People who'd lost enough money or won enough, without waiting for the rest of the card, were making their way out. Cars were moving, and there was the usual impatient hornblowing. I dodged the moving vehicles, heading for the Chev. Then there was a new sound, the sound of a woman screaming. I looked around and quickly found the source. An elderly woman, pressed against a cream colored Buick, and drowning out all the automobiles with a steady high-pitched wail. People began to make for her, and plenty got there ahead of me. From the back of a tense ring of horrified onlookers I got another look at my friend of the many-hued outfit. He was crouched on all fours between two automobiles. His back was towards me, and planted in between his shoulder blades was an ice-pick, driven home with deadly strength and precision. He hadn't bled much, just a red circle the size of a dollar piece all around the shaft of the pick. Now he moved, groping blindly towards the nearest car. The bony fingers touched metal and he turned himself somehow, and began to pull himself upright. Along from me, a woman fainted. Nobody paid any heed as she crumpled to the ground. Rainbow was almost on his feet now, fighting every desperate inch of his way up the car body. Upright at last, he eased weight off his fingers a pound at a time. Now he was on his own two feet, half-facing the spot where I was standing. Not that he was seeing me. I'd seen that glazed look on too many faces before. Rainbow was all through seeing anybody. There was a gasp from the crowd as he essayed a pace forward. One knee began very slowly to cave. The little man held out a hand as though appealing for someone to help him. Then he pitched headlong against the bonnet of the car.

'His face,' a woman screamed. 'His poor face.'

As he went down, his face smashed into a silver metal goddess that someone had fixed to the hood. It didn't matter much. He was dead before he tried to walk, the whole thing was purely a reflex action. There were uniforms now, sweating men in khaki shirts pushing their way forward and ordering everybody around. They weren't real cops, just track police, but that gave them badges and guns. It was no place for an innocent bystander to linger, I decided. They were beginning to single out witnesses now, and there were plenty available without me. I edged away fast, and just in time. The track boys had cordoned off thirty or forty people, and if I knew anything those people could kiss the next three hours goodbye.

I unlocked the Chev thoughtfully, and climbed in. For some reason, the murder of the little guy was getting to me in a personal way. There was no reason why it should. No reason at all. I'd promised him I'd be back in five minutes, and I'd done exactly that, give a minute or two. No reason for me to face anything at all. Why, I didn't even know the man, never set eyes on him before. Yeah, said some other voice inside, but he knew you all

11

right. He wanted you, wanted your help. I blared my horn at some character who tried to slice the nose off my car as I wheeled for the exit gates. He scowled at me and blared right back. I felt temper rising, and hoped he'd climb out and make something of it. I hoped — childish, I reasoned. All you want to do is sock somebody, anybody, because of what happened to a total stranger who was color-blind. I waved the other driver on his way, and he nodded with quick triumph.

On the highway back to the city I had a sudden thought. The little man had been in the car — why did he leave it incidentally? — still he'd been inside. I felt quickly under the dash to see whether a certain article of property was missing, but my fingers found it. Taped tightly on the underside a derringer single shot pistol which I liked to have around for unexpected visitors. About to draw my hand away, I felt something else. It was unfamiliar, and it certainly didn't belong to me. There was momentary panic in my mind as I considered a possible bomb, but I dismissed that quickly. Why would anybody want to be rid of me at the moment. Not that I didn't have any enemies. You don't make a living the way I do without people wishing you were dead. But right then I hadn't anybody who was stirred up enough to blow me to pieces. Nobody, I amended, who wasn't in the penitentiary.

No, this was something else, something put there by the little guy during those few minutes while I placed a bet. He knew those people were getting close, and so he got rid of — what? Probably the very thing they wanted to take away from him. And if he'd thoughtfully palmed it on to me, then I might be in the market for the latest type of back-decoration. I gave the heap some more gas and got into the city fast. Outside the office, I pulled in and cut the motor. Checking guiltily around to be sure no-one was close, I tugged at the thing and it came away in my hand.

'Hi Mr. Preston.'

I turned quickly to find a cheery blond kid standing by the open car window.

'Oh, hi Luke. How's the job?'

'Fine, thanks. Just fine. Say, did you hurt your hand?'

He nodded towards my left hand carefully hidden under the dash, with whatever it was resting on the palm. I grinned feebly

'No, er — why no. Arm gets a little stiff sometimes. The doc says I have to hold it out in front of me like this with the fingers outstretched.'

He was all concern.

'Really? Say, that sounds like my Uncle Olaf. He has this, what is it, muscular trouble, you know? I just remembered, he has this stuff he rubs on. Maybe it would help you. I'll get the name of it for you, huh?'

'Well, that's nice of you Luke, but this is nothing. Really. It's always better after a couple of minutes.'

He shook his head.

'You don't have to tell me, Mr. Preston, I've seen Uncle Olaf when it stiffens up. Say, I'll be glad to do it.'

I wished Luke would go away. And his Uncle Olaf. I wished Luke and his Uncle

Olaf in a very uncomfortable place. But he had offered a way to get rid of him.

'That's nice of you Luke,' I repeated. 'Say could you do it now? I'll be up in my office.'

He grinned widely.

'You bet. Consider it done.'

And at last he was gone. I pulled my hand quickly into view and stuffed it into my pocket. Then I locked up and went into the building.

Florence Digby sat primly behind her typewriter banging away with that mathematical precision of hers. She looked very cool in the crisp blue blouse. The look she gave me over the machine was cool, too.

'Why, Mr. Preston, how nice. I didn't think we'd be seeing you again today. Did the track blow up?'

'Ha, ha,' I told her. 'If you must know, I quit while I was ahead. I picked up two hundred and fifty on the fifth alone.'

But Florence was not to be fooled that easily. Smiling sweetly she asked.

'And how much did you lose on the first four?'

I walked across to my own door.

'Any messages?'

Rebuffed, she stared down at the pad beside her.

'Two fifteen, a Mr. Rendell. I told him you'd be back later. He wouldn't leave a message. Two forty, Mr. Rendell again. Finally, at three five, he sounded so excited I told him where you were. I knew you wouldn't be pleased, but the poor man said it was absolutely vital he should see you right away. He said something about going out there to find you. Did he do that?'

My fingers clenched around the thing in my pocket.

'No,' I said. 'I didn't see anybody. Lot of people out there.'

'I see. Well, in that case, if he missed you at the track, he said he'd call tonight.'

I made a face.

'Well I certainly hope you didn't let him think I was going to hang around here waiting?'

'Not at all. He said he had your home number too.'

I looked at Florence suspiciously.

'Do you mean he already had it, or you gave it to him?'

The small mouth set very straight.

'Mr. Preston, that was quite uncalled for. I believe you perfectly well know I would never do such a thing. He knew the number.'

We were even. I went inside and closed the door. At last I was able to take my first look at whatever was in my pocket. I pulled it out and put it on the table in front of me. There was no mystery about the wrapping paper. It was a good old-fashioned fifty dollar bill, wrapped in a loose oblong and held in place by a thick band of elastic. I pulled off the band and smoothed out the bill. Inside was a pad of cotton waste. When I pulled this to pieces I found a small key. The key was marked Monkton City Express Company and was stamped with the number twenty-three. I dropped the cotton pad into the waste-basket, then the band. That left two articles on the table, one banknote and one key. The Express crowd ran a deposit box service on a twenty-four hour rental, and key 23 was like many I'd seen before. After some involved thinking, I decided I'd been hired. The fee was fifty bucks and to earn it I had to get hold of whatever was tucked away in the deposit box. That much seemed fairly clear. After that it was hazy. Presumably the guy who hired me was the little man who just bled to death in the parking lot out at the track. So, if I collected the contents of box 23, where did I deliver it? I could study the newspapers till they mentioned his family, then hand it over to them. On the other hand, I might not be doing them any favor at all. The contents might be liable to blow up in their faces. It wasn't likely, for example, that the man's life savings were in that box. Somebody wanted the stuff badly enough to kill him for it. If it was only money, or something else readily negotiable, there wouldn't be any point to killing him for the key. In those circumstances, the smart thing to do would be to let him open the box himself, take whatever was inside, and then kill him later and remove the cash or whatever. That would be the smart thing, and whoever killed him was almost

18

certainly a professional. The pro has a great regard for ice-picks. Amateurs usually go for something more showy. Then there was the way the pick had been used, straight in and driven home hard. Amateurs always strike downwards, which is a good way to wound a man, and maybe even kill him eventually if you hit the right spot. But that kind of blow leaves a man plenty of time for last words, and one thing no professional ever chances is a dying declaration. So my many-colored acquaintance had been bumped off good, and it seemed likely the reason was the piece of shaped metal lying on my table.

Having almost, but not entirely, elimi-nated the money theory, I had to assume there was something else of value, even though the value might not be realised on an open market. Value is a funny commodity. There are many things in this world highly prized by their owners, or perhaps by a certain body of people for particular reasons. In a free market these things may not be worth a plugged nickel. A photograph of a departed relative, a souvenir from the war, any war. Letters, diplomas, personal things of that kind. Most of the owners would go to some lengths to recover such items. But not very many would plant an ice-pick in a man's back.

The sensible thing was obvious. I ought to send the key to the police department and the fifty bucks anonymously to the little man's family. But I haven't always been famous for doing the sensible thing. Plus, I have this tremendous curiosity, which some might call nosiness. On top of all that, I had every right to consider myself hired by the dead man. I decided on a variant of the sensible thing. First, I'd see what was in the box. Then, if it seemed the proper thing to do, I'd hand *that* over to the law.

Congratulating myself on this facile compromise, I buzzed for Miss Digby.

'It's getting late, Mr. Preston,' was her entry line.

'I appreciate that. Like you to do one more thing before you go home.'

I handed over the key and told her I wanted the contents of the box.

She gave me one of those Digby looks, which this time was asking why I couldn't do it myself.

'I'd go myself,' I explained, 'But I promised to take a call from San Fransisco in exactly four minutes. Hope you don't mind.'

'Very well. What is in the box Mr. Preston? I trust it won't be very heavy?'

I admitted I had no idea, but stressed the importance of my getting hold of it as soon as possible. She left then, and I dialled Sam Thompson's number.

'Preston,' I announced.

The groan at the other end confirmed I had the right man.

'Sam, I want you to get over to the Express Company right now. Florence Digby is on her way to empty a deposit box. Watch her, only really watch her. If anybody so much as looks at her twice go after him hard.'

'If it's like that, why send a woman?' he demanded.

Sam has this knack for asking uncomfortable questions.

'They may know me. I don't think so,

21

but it's a possibility. I don't believe there's a remote chance they'll know Florence.'

'Then why call me?'

'Because it's Florence, Sam. And with her I don't take even the most remote chance.'

That was good enough.

'I'm on my way. If it's all right, I'll come to your office ten minutes after she gets back.'

'Be extra careful,' I warned.

Then I sat back and waited. In twenty minutes or thereabouts I should know a lot more about why guys in panama hats were wearing ice-picks this year. Idly, I wondered whether the little guy had been the Rendell who was chasing me, or whether I had another possible client about to make contact.

I stared out of the window at the small section of the Pacific Ocean which qualifies my office for the description panoramic view of the Pacific, and a proportionately higher rental. The old girl looked pretty good in the late afternoon sun, small white flecks of foam on the calm blue, and some young swimmers having a whale of a time with surfing boards. It would be nice to be a young beach bum, with nothing to worry about except the way your tan looked, and your chances with the little dark one in the red one-piece. The outer door opened, and Florence came in quickly. I was relieved to see her, Thompson or no.

'There it is, Mr. Preston. Not very impressive.'

She dumped a small parcel on the table. It certainly was not very impressive. It had the external appearance of being a slim bundle of papers. Whatever it was, it was wrapped in a yellow waterproof cover. I looked at it and wondered. Florence Digby stood across the table, trying not to look impatient.

'Well?' she demanded finally.

'Thank you, Miss Digby. I'm obliged to you.'

I even smiled. But she was not so easily deterred.

'Well, aren't you going to open it?' she queried.

'Eh? Oh, no. I'm not supposed to do that. I merely collect it from the Express

Company, then deliver it somewhere else. Sorry, no opening ceremony.' She was as disappointed as any other woman would be, who'd collected a mysterious package and was then not to be permitted to view the contents.

'Oh. Then if there's nothing further —?'

There was nothing further. I watched her go out, heard the door close. After that I gave her one clear minute to come back for anything she may have left behind. I had a very good reason for not opening the package in her presence. If I wasn't mistaken, the package had already been the cause of murder. I didn't want her to know what was inside. That way she would know nothing, and that would be a very good insurance against anyone who didn't want people knowing things. Time was up. I picked up the little bundle and inspected it carefully. The oilskin was fastened with paper tape. It seemed to be parcels day for Preston. Carefully, I peeled off one piece of the tape making sure not to cause any damage. I was

hunched right over the thing, concen-
trating on what I was doing.

'Put it down.'

I looked up. There was a man standing
there with a Colt 38 in his hand.

2

I put down the bundle. I always do what people tell me. Especially people who hold artillery in my direction. The man was about fifty years old, and he'd packed a lot of trouble into those years. He wore a dark seaman's jersey and stained pants. And he'd held a gun before.

'Don't bother to knock,' I told him.

'People always complain about the way I behave,' he told me. 'Just for instance, you take now. Here I'm talking all nice and friendly, you make one little move and blooey — I blow off half your shoulder. Does that sound like a nice guy?'

I shook my head.

'Not especially. You sound like a real nasty guy to me.'

He beamed, and the smile was not unattractive.

'That's me,' he agreed. 'You got me dead to rights. I am a real nasty guy. So don't make me shoot this thing off, huh, joker?'

I didn't want him to shoot that thing off. What I wanted was for him to go on talking in that flat Eastern twang.

'You have the floor,' I assured him. 'And no, I do not wish to be shot.'

His eyes glinted.

'Smart,' he decided. 'With smart people I can always do business. This' — he tapped at the revolver — 'this is really for the dumb ones.'

'Fine, fine,' I said heartily. 'Well now, what can I do for you, Mr. — ?'

The gun waved impatiently, and I stopped talking quite suddenly. Because one thing was for certain. This one would squeeze that small piece of metal crooked in his right forefinger. He would do it without hesitation.

'You know what I want. Slide it across.'

I looked amazed, and tapped at the yellow oilskin.

'You came for this? But how could you possibly know I had it?'

He smiled again, pleased with himself.

'Cute, ain't I? Well, there's no harm to

it. I seen Race put the thing away, so I knew where to look. All I had to do was hang around. I seen the dame come in, followed her when she left. She headed straight for you, joker. When I saw what it said on the door outside, I knew I was in business. I waited a couple minutes, the dame comes out. She hadn't got that beauty with her, so it had to be in here. Simple?'

'Very simple. But suppose I don't want to give it to you?'

He sighed, and the knuckle of his finger turned very slightly white. I did something similar.

'Give yourself a break, and don't mess in this,' he warned. 'If you'd opened that thing, I'd have rubbed you out like a bluebottle fly. Way things are, there ain't need for you to come to no harm. Act smart.'

Behind him in the open doorway loomed the large and comforting figure of Sam Thompson.

'Suppose I told you there's a friend of mine standing right behind you?' I said.

He sneered with exasperation.

'I'm supposed to turn around and give you a chance at my back. Listen, I got advice for this friend. He ought to give it to me good, and right now.'

I shrugged.

'You're calling it. You heard what the man said, Sam.'

Thompson double chopped with those big hands at the sides of my visitor's neck. He went down without a sound, like a poleaxed steer. Thompson bent over and picked up the gun. I ran a hand round inside my collar. It came away damp.

'Brother, am I glad to see you,' I told him.

'You should be. This is a mean looking face. Who is he?'

'I don't know,' I admitted. 'You ever see him before?'

The big man nodded.

'Sure, else what are you paying me for? I spotted this guy tail Miss Digby away from the Express office. He wasn't doing any harm, so I kind of tagged along behind. He came up here, then waited till she left. That was his cue.'

'It was yours, too,' I pointed out. 'What

took you so long?'

'No gun. If I was coming in, it had to be very, very quiet. And that takes time when there's a door to open.'

'You certainly took plenty of it,' I complained. 'While you were busy being very very quiet, I coulda been very very dead.'

Sam's homely face broke into a grin.

'Ah, stop bleeding. Nobody got hurt. What do we do with him?'

'First of all, let's see if he'll tell us anything.'

I went through his pockets and found one ignition key and thirty five cents.

'Travels light, don't he?' remarked Thompson.

'Yeah.'

I probed around at the thick sweater, and felt something hard underneath. Rolling up the wool I came out with a calf billfold. It contained a driver's licence made out to Julian Ventura and a thick wad of bills amounting to several thousand dollars. There was also a business card for somebody called Tapper Holland, Vodvil's Leading Dancer. The card was yellow with age.

'We could keep the money for damage to the carpet,' suggested Thompson.

'Uh, uh. That wouldn't be honest,' I negatived. Then a thought struck me. 'On the other hand, this guy has to be some kind of an operator. Right?'

'Right.'

'And what is the one thing an operator cannot be without if he is going to operate?'

Sam's eyes gleamed.

'I'm ahead of you. We remove the grease, and some of the wheels get stuck.'

'You have it Sam.'

I lifted out the sheaf of bills and stuffed them in my pocket. Then I rolled up the sweater again, and put the billfold back. Mr. Julian Ventura showed no sign of waking up.

'What do we do now?' asked Thompson.

'We find out about this guy. All we can. You go and wait outside for him to leave. Does he have a car?'

'Drives a last year's Olds. It's out front.'

'You have the advantage because he

didn't see who hit him. Tail him, and watch out for yourself. You better beat it, he's coming round. See you at Dino's at eight.'

Sam went out quickly. I went to a drawer and dropped the oilskin bundle inside. There was a wheezing noise from the floor. My visitor shook his head several times and sat upright. His eyes focussed on my feet, then travelled up to my face. He shook his head sadly, and began to stand up, massaging tenderly at his neck.

'First time I've ever known that friend gag to work,' he grumbled.

'Oh, it works fine if you remember to have the friend behind the other guy.'

He looked at me strangely.

'Let me give you some advice, joker. Give me that package, and I'll blow. You can have my word you won't be bothered any more.'

'That's advice?' I demanded. 'But I'm the one with the gun. Look.'

I held up the Colt so he could see it. It didn't seem to create much of an impression.

'Pah,' he grimaced. 'What about it? You ain't gonna kill me. That means as much to me as a candy bar. How about what I said?'

I marvelled at his coolness.

'Suppose I had the package, which I don't, why would I give it to you?'

The deep eyes narrowed.

'That's on the level? You don't have it any more?'

'Not any more. My friend took it away with him. It seems to bring the wrong kind of people into the office.'

Ventura sighed and shook his head.

'You're all kinds of a fool, Preston. I was levelling before. If you handed that thing over, you'da been clean. Now you're just a walking corpse.'

There was something so offhand in the calm certainty of his tone that I felt something cold crawl up my spine.

'What's your name?' I asked.

'Go to hell.'

He turned and shambled towards the door.

'Hold it.'

He looked around at me and the gun.

'Well?'

'I'm going to hand you over to the law,' I informed him.

He chuckled then, a fruity sound that did not match the quiet malevolence in his eyes.

'What did I do? Park in front of a hydrant?'

'I can think of at least four charges,' I replied evenly.

Ventura looked me over coolly, then spat on the floor.

'That's probably five,' he sneered. 'Don't shout copper at me, Preston. You don't want any coppers pushing their ugly faces into this. Too many people in this already, and nobody wants the blue boys. And the guy who holds the package, he wants them less than anybody else. And that guy is you. Go to hell.'

And with that he showed me his back again and went out. I thought I'd handled it nicely. A little bluff, little bluster, a little fear. Though I had an uncomfortable feeling not all the fear had been phoney. There was an assurance about Julian Ventura that did nothing for upset stomachs. It isn't every day you meet a man who walks away from a pointed gun as though he hadn't noticed it.

I went out and locked the entrance door. As a man who didn't have long to live, I couldn't use any more unannounced visitors. Plus, it was time I had a good look at the cause of my untimely decease. Taking the package from the drawer, I peeled off the rest of the adhesive tape and unwrapped the yellow oilskin. There was a small bundle of papers inside. On top was an envelope which had been mailed to J. Holland at a New York address. The date stamp was smudged but the year was clear enough, 1942. There was nothing inside. Next was a photostat of a marriage license. The principals were Joseph Holland and Molly Krasner, and the marriage took place in New Jersey in 1939. Beneath that was a much-creased clipping from some yellow sheet. The glaring tabloid style told a sensational story about the murder of a Bronx housewife by her jealous husband. When you cut out all the suggestive material, the facts were few and familiar.

Joseph Holland, 24, known throughout the world of variety as Tapper Holland, had caught his wife Molly in bed with another man not named. Holland had gone berserk and attacked the pair of them. The man got away, and was still being sought by the authorities, who did not know his identity. Molly was not so lucky. In trying to get away from her husband she fell down the stairs and broke her neck, dying a few minutes later. Their two year old baby was being cared for by relatives. There was no date-line on the story, and it didn't say what happened to Holland, because the trial was still in progress. There was a picture of Molly, a good-looking brunette with unusually large eyes. There was a picture of Holland too, one of those all black and white flashlight pictures that could be anybody. He seemed to have black hair, and sported a thick mustache and about four days growth of beard. Any jury would have convicted the guy on that picture alone. Then there was a postcard size picture of Molly Holland holding a baby in her arms. She certainly had been a good-looking girl, enough to spark off the kind of trouble that ended her life. On the back of the picture was the name of the photographer and the legend '1946 series'. So it seemed likely that Molly had died in 1947 or at the latest 1948. The last paper in the pile was a many-folded theater display bill. It was from the Palace Theater Broadway, no less, for a week in March 1938. Three spots up from the bottom was Tapper Holland and Molly — Grace and Movement.

I pushed the papers away from me and lit up an Old Favorite. I don't know what I'd been expecting to find, but it hadn't been anything like this. There'd probably been a bit of a stir back in 1947 or whenever, but all this stuff amounted to now was so much waste-paper. Except maybe to relatives, who could have some sentimental wish to keep some of it. But sentimental relatives do not prowl race-tracks with ice-picks in their pockets. Neither do they tote Colt .38s in pursuit of their personal treasures. Well, I wasn't going to make any progress sitting around. Best get out and around where there are people. If it's information you need, you have to have people, and I was in great need of plenty. Refolding the package, I sealed it in a buff envelope, and addressed it to Sam Thompson, General Delivery, Monkton City. Then I put the thing inside my coat.

Ventura's cash was still in a side pocket. Now I took it out and counted it. There were four thousand seven hundred dollars in the wad plus a few odd bills. The money was a nuisance. I didn't want it, but I also didn't want Ventura to have it. For the moment I shoved it back in my pocket. Then I got ready to leave and opened the outer door. As I did so a very large man blocked my exit.

'Oh no,' I groaned. 'The day hasn't been tough enough.'

'Nice to see you too, Preston.'

The very large man ambled into the office. His name was Randall, Gil Randall. That was his personal name. His official name was Sergeant Randall of the Monkton City Police Department, Homicide Bureau. If I have to see the guy, and I avoid it whenever possible, I like to go into the encounter fully fit. Like say a week on a steady diet, plenty of fresh air, and sleep. Because Randall is at his best all the time, and his best is very very good. It's bad enough trying to fool the man any time but to try it when you're not one hundred per cent on the ball is plain foolish.

'Always liked your office. It's neat. Neat, and it has style without being fancy. Know what I mean?'

He turned the sleepy eyes in my direction. That's another thing I complain about with the big policeman, those eyes. You'd swear the guy was half-asleep, or part-stoned, or maybe just not very bright. You would be wrong, on all three counts.

'Look, Gil, if you want to rent an office I'll be glad to take it up with the company. Was there anything else?'

'Kinda jumpy today aren't we? Maybe we've been breaking one or two small laws?' he asked hopefully.

'Nothing worth your attention,' I assured him. 'A little arson, rape, one or two homicides. The usual daily run. You know how it is.'

'Sure.'

He stared all around the office again, then poked his head inside the inner room.

'Nice in there, too,' he remarked. 'Even better in there. Why, a man could just sit and think up all kinds of illegal dodges. No?'

'I have to make a living.'

I wished he'd go away. Randall is trouble any time, but right now I was a walking jail-sentence. In one pocket I had close to five thousand dollars I'd stolen, technically. In another I had a whole heap of documents I couldn't begin to explain. And tucked under my arm was a gun for which I had no license, and which probably had a police history three feet long. You might say I was slightly vulnerable. Randall smiled in that friendly fashion of his.

'Glad you're all set to confess.'

'Glad you're glad. What did I do?' I asked suspiciously.

'Leave out the rest for now,' he suggested. 'Let's just stay with the homicides.'

'Could you narrow it down?'

'Anything for an old suspect. Let's make it just one homicide. Now you can't object to that, Preston. What's one teeny old murder to you?'

'Nothing,' I admitted. 'Who did I kill?'

He wagged a finger the size of a two-dollar cigar.

'Memory, memory,' he reproved. 'Think back. Back to the fifth race.'

'Which track?' I countered.

'C'm on Preston, be nice. I had a hard day too. Soon as I get you locked up, I can go home and have a cold beer. A man was killed today in the parking lot out at Palmtrees. I have two witnesses who place you at the scene.'

I made a face.

'As bad as that? Lead me to the gas chamber.'

Randall didn't lose his temper. He seldom does.

'Little early for that. Everything in good time. Right now I'd as soon lead you downtown for one or two questions, unless you prefer to answer them here.'

The way he said it sounded harmless

enough. What he was telling me was that I could either be nice, or spend several frustrating hours down at headquarters. With the stuff I was carrying, I probably wouldn't see the outside again for years.

'All right,' I said resignedly. 'I was at the track.'

'In the parking lot,' he added.

'In the parking lot,' I agreed.

'Who was the guy?' he demanded.

I tried to look like a man who is anxious to clear a misunderstanding.

'I don't know. Look Gil, I went to play the races. After the fifth I won a few dollars, and I have sense enough to quit when I'm ahead. When I went for my car there was a crowd gathering. I went to take a look at what was going on. There was this guy. Somebody had stuck an ice-pick in him. The uniforms blew in, I blew out. That's all there is.'

He never took his eyes off my face.

'Did you see who killed your buddy?'

'You're wasting your time, I never saw that guy before.'

'Then what were you doing there?' he asked.

'I told you. There must have been thirty or forty other people there. Why pick on me?'

He sucked noisily at a tooth.

'There were forty three people there to be precise. All citizens. Why pick on you? I'll tell you. These other people were harmless. They never even saw a murder before. That makes them different from you. But here's the clincher. They stayed. They didn't dive in their cars and beat it. You did that. Why?'

I looked amazed.

'You can't be serious. Real cops are bad enough, but you don't honestly think I'd let myself be grabbed by those imitation policemen out at the tracks? Once they found out who I was, they'd have probably beaten me half to death before you guys even arrived.'

I was aiming deliberately at a weak spot. Randall doesn't have many of those, but he was a policeman, a real one. And one thing that sticks in the craw of a real cop, is the mention of all those organisation police forces with which our fair country is blessed. The big man

43

nodded despite himself.

'I know what you mean. I don't like amateurs any way, but amateurs with badges are the worst kind. You should have seen what those guys did to the set-up out there. They planted their big feet every which way. Whatever there might have been for us to find, those guys trampled it out of existence in five minutes flat. That's on the level, huh?'

The question slid in so casually at the end, I almost missed it.

'Eh? Huh? Oh, on the level. Sure. Exactly the way I told you. What have you got so far?'

'I'm asking the questions,' he roared. Then, quite suddenly he changed his tone. 'Ah, what am I making so much noise for? I just dropped around making a routine check on anybody who was out there today. I don't imagine you really had anything to do with it. Fact is Preston, the captain is like an elephant with tusk-ache. I wasn't kidding about that bunch of comic coppers. They fouled the whole scene up good, and my respected captain is not making life too comfortable for us all right this minute.'

'He can be a tough one,' I agreed. 'But it looked like a pro-job, huh?'

The sergeant made a face.

'Sure. It looked like a pro-job. But that doesn't have to mean it was done by a pro. Not these days. One time of day guys had to learn their trade by experience. Experience comes expensive, and every time they made a little mistake they picked up a little time with it. Everybody was happy. The wrong guys got tougher and smarter, and the sentences got longer. The law enforcement agencies knew who they were, where they were and how they operated. You got to look at a job and say, 'Charlie the Gimp did this,' or 'Find out where Roses McCarthy was last night'.'

Randall sighed dolefully and looked at me.

'I don't get it,' I admitted. 'What's different now? Except you have a crime lab as well to back you up.'

'Sure,' he conceded, 'We have those guys, the saints be praised. Only we don't know where to start looking half the time.

Because the public has its own Crime University of the Air. Every trick in the book regularly pushed across in glowing detail from every television network in the country. Even the honest people know as much about criminal methods today as the average crook knew twenty years ago. That's what I mean. So it looked like a pro job, but it could have been your cousin Emily's first little venture for all I know.'

'Except I don't have a cousin Emily.'

He brightened, and said:

'Progress, yet. At least I can scratch her.'

We talked some more, and he asked a few routine questions about what I'd seen of the little man's death. He was satisfied with what I told him, or seemed to be. With Randall it never pays to assume too much. As he was getting ready to leave, I asked:

'Who was the little fellow anyhow? I never saw him before.'

'Name of Rendell. We don't have his first name yet, but everybody knew him as Race.'

46

Race Rendell. Well that took care of my prospective client. Except that he was one already, in a roundabout way.

'Race?' I repeated thoughtfully. 'Sounds like a racing guy, but I don't recall I ever saw him out there before today.'

'Maybe you didn't. Only one or two of the guards knew him. It was the trainers and the bookies who told us about him. Mostly he operates up north, makes an occasional trip in our direction.'

'Sounds like a nice wide field you have to cover,' I suggested. 'These racing killings are a dime a dozen, aren't they?'

'You're telling it. What with crooked trainers, hold-back jockeys, dopers, chiselling bookies, the field is wide open all right. I had one like this a coupla years back. A lulu. It turned out half the people at the track were waiting for the right moment to rub out the other half.'

I tried to sound encouraging.

'Well, don't feel too bad,' I soothed. 'At least you can be sure it was nothing to do with this city.'

The big man raised his eyebrows.

'I can? And even if you're right how do

47

you mean I needn't feel too bad? You're talking like a real private john now. What do you mean, nothing to do with this city. It's our track, isn't it?'

'Sure, but — .'

'But nothing. We should put up a sign out at Palmtrees? Off limits to the city police. Perform your murders here? Everything is our business, everything, and don't go thinking otherwise.'

'My error,' I bowed.

'Damn right.' He glowered at me, like a wounded professional. 'Well, I can't stand around here chinning with you all night. Drop around some time tomorrow and sign your statement.'

Still bristling with offended dignity he went out. I breathed a sigh of relief, and got out of there before any more unwelcome visitors arrived.

I mailed the bulky envelope and put Ventura's money in the night-safe on my way back to Parkside Towers. There I changed my clothes, slipping on fresh linen after the heat of the day. While dressing, I had a can of cold beer and watched a local newscast. There was a lot of talk about the

48

Rendell murder, but none of it meant anything. They also carried pictures of Palmtrees, in case nobody ever saw a race-track before, and some loving closeups of the parking lot, busy with police both in and out of uniform. What it all added up to was that Race Rendell — colorful race-track figure — had been done to death in that very space, and nobody had the faintest idea what it was all about. I switched the thing off and emptied the last of the beer. Then I sat around, killing time and wondering exactly what I was getting mixed up in. I was so deep in thought, the noise of the phone made me jump.

'Mr. Preston? It's me, Johnny Lugio.'

At once I was glad I picked up the phone. Lugio worked at the track.

'Hi Johnny, what's new?'

'Listen, Mr. Preston, I got to see you.'

I didn't want to seem too anxious.

'I'm pretty busy tonight. How 'bout tomorrow?'

'Not tomorrow.' His voice became urgent. 'Look, it has to be now.'

I checked my watch. It was eight twenty.

'I have a date at nine,' I told him. 'Where are you?'

'I'm at the Jockeys Joint. You know, on 14th?'

'It's off my route Johnny. I could only stay five minutes. What's it all about?'

'Can't talk much on the 'phone. You understand. It has to do with, er — you know, that thing happened out there today.'

Keeping my voice flat I replied.

'I don't see what that has to do with me, boy. But if you say so, O.K. Five minutes I'll be there, five minutes I stay.'

'See you.'

I did a couple of dance-steps after hanging up. Johnny Lugio was a one-time jockey. After he had a bad fall one time, I helped get him a news stand to keep him eating till he was really fit again. Turned out to be a good idea too, because his leg never really did heal up properly. Once he realised he'd never get on a horse again, he settled for stable work or anything else that would keep him around the horses. But he never forgot the three or four guys who set up that stand, and I had been one of them. So whatever he wanted to tell me, it would be on the level and it would be free. I finished the Astaire imitation by tripping over my own feet, and headed for the door.

3

The Jockeys Joint is one of those rare places that means what it says. There you will find jockeys old and new, little men with big hearts and enough stories to put a fisherman to shame. In addition to the jockeys you will find people who either need or like to be around the little men. Trainers, stable-hands, owners sometimes, and a flock of track-lovers who prefer to do their drinking with the people who are going to lose their shirts for them the following day. The place always smells of horse-liniment and cigars, and tonight was no exception. The noise was deafening.

Lugio waved from a corner table, and I went over to shake hands.

'Hi Johnny. Long time.'

'Too long, Mr. Preston. You oughta get around more.'

He had his own bottle and he poured me out a slug. To me it smelled like liniment and I said so. The little guy chuckled.

'Everything in this place smells the same.' He showed me the label of a drinkable bourbon.

'In that case, mud in yours,' I told him.

He was right. It wasn't liniment at all. The formalities over, I looked at my watch.

'That's on the level about my date,' I told him. 'Five minutes is tops. Can we get to it.'

'Sure.'

He looked carefully around to be sure no one was listening. As a precaution it was slightly superfluous. You could have fired off a moon rocket and it wouldn't have been heard at the other end of the room.

'It's about this guy who got bumped off today,' he muttered.

'I heard about it,' I nodded.

'Funny thing, he'd been trying to get in touch with you,' he told me.

'With me?' I was puzzled. 'Why would he want to do that?'

Suddenly he had my full attention.

Plus. He shook his head.

'I wouldn't know about that. He wouldn't tell me.'

I put a hand on his arm.

'We're not getting any place, Johnny. Let's start over. You knew this guy — er — what was his name?'

'Rendell. Race Rendell. Sure I knew him. From when I was up there back in the old days. You know?'

I knew. And I didn't want a flood of reminiscences to get started.

'O.K. You knew him.'

'He didn't come down this way much. Usually stuck to the bigger tracks. I first saw him down here about three years ago. That was about the time I found out about this.'

He slapped at his twisted leg and looked at it thoughtfully.

'That was a rotten break you got there,' I said sympathetically. 'So you ran into him out at Palmtrees.'

'Like I said. Well we chewed the fat about old times. He told me he made a lot of money on my rides and he was sorry I was out of the game. You know, the usual. We had a few beers, and I said to him, I didn't know he ever made it to Palmtrees. Know what he told me?'

I shook my head.

'He told me he always came down once in a year to see an old friend. I didn't think anything of it, why would I? After that, sure enough, he'd turn up each year. He'd always look me up, and we'd have a drink and a tongue fest. I'd ask him how his friend was and he'd say oh fine, fine, and that would be that. But I always knew he didn't want to talk about his friend. You know? Sometimes you can tell about these things. People don't come right out and say mind your own business, but they let you know they don't want to talk about it. That's how it was with Race and this friend of his.'

'So he was here on this yearly trip when he got murdered?'

'No. I'm coming to that. He came two months ago. We had our usual visit, and when he went off I didn't expect him again till next year. You shoulda seen my face when the guy turned up yesterday.'

'Yesterday. You're sure of that?'

'Sure I'm sure. That's a funny question. How could I be wrong about a thing like that?' queried Johnny, his tone injured.

'Sorry. Please go on.'

'Well, you coulda bowled me over with a battleship. Naturally, I asked the guy what it was all about. Was his friend sick maybe? He clammed up on that quick and told me no, there were a couple of special nags he was following around.'

It was evident from his tone that the ex-jockey hadn't believed him.

'You didn't go for that, huh?'

'I did not. I was insulted a guy would feed me a yarn like that. You see Mr. Preston, there's all kinds of guys play the ponies for a living. They got all kinds of systems. There's pin guys, numbers guys, short-price guys, there's dozens of 'em. But one thing they never do, not the system boys. They never change the system, but never. They may shake it around a little, pretty it up, but it's always the same system.'

He looked at me as though it was my turn to speak. I spoke.

'This is leading us somewhere?'

'Natch. Race was a jockey man, get it? He'd have this bunch of riders and they'd carry his money for the season.'

Now I was getting aboard.

'But he told you he was following certain horses. That would mean he'd changed his system, and that's not possible.'

'Right,' agreed Johnny, with animation. 'Because if he ever did change his system, which is the next thing to a miracle, he woulda told me all about it. He wouldn't be able to help it, it'd be like growing another arm.'

'It means something else, too,' I mused.

'Whassat?'

'It means that if Rendell would tell you a cockeyed tale like that, he must have been upset. Either very upset or worried about something. Too worried to think what he was saying.'

'Sure. I figured that. And what else would he be worried about but this friend?'

It seemed a reasonable deduction, I looked at the one-time jockey.

'Why're you telling me all this, Johnny?

57

Seems to me the police would be better able to use it.'

He dropped his eyes and toyed with the glass.

'I'm coming to it. You see, when Race blew in yesterday, I figured he'd meet me here last night, same like always. He didn't show. Well, he never said he'd be here, so I figured he had some place else to go. Like maybe his friend was sick, or in a jam. O.K.?'

'With you so far.'

'Then today, he comes to the track looking for me. I used to tell him how you and those other guys helped me that time. In fact,' he grinned, 'sometimes I used to think I told that story too many times. Still and all, Race knew all about it. So today, when he found me, it was you he wanted to know about.'

'Me?'

'Yeah. He said he needed somebody in your line of business, somebody he could trust. From what I'd told him all those years, he figured you might be the guy. He wouldn't tell me what it was all about. So I said, 'look Race, I don't know what kinda trouble you got, so how do I know whether Mr. Preston will help you? But,' I says, 'he is a guy you can talk to. If he can help you he will. If he can't he won't go running to the johns.' You see, Mr. Preston I had it figured the kind of trouble he was in, would likely be police kind of trouble.'

'It often is,' I confirmed. I was beginning to feel slightly uneasy.

'Well like I said, after we had this talk, Race goes off to call your office. He tried a couple times, maybe three, I don't know. Then he comes back to me and says you're at the track. Could I put a finger on you.'

Now I knew why I'd had that feeling.

'And you did.'

I made it a statement of fact. Lugio nodded.

'I did. You were over near the winner's enclosure. Not a big crowd today. I spotted you under half an hour.'

This had all the makings of a blackmail opening. But from Lugio I couldn't believe it, or didn't want to. I swallowed a mouthful of my drink and stuck an Old

59

Favorite in my face. Race Rendell had been looking for me. He found me, and was promptly murdered. I had already told the police the man was a total stranger. The little man sitting opposite knew that wasn't true. People disappoint me every day, but I never imagined Johnny Lugio would join the happy band.

'Let's have the punch line, Johnny. I have to leave.'

He fiddled unnecessarily with his glass, as though embarrassed. He had every right to be, I reflected sourly.

'What happened when Race spoke to you? Did he tell you anything?'

'No,' I replied shortly. 'He said he wanted to talk. I told him to wait in the parking lot. That was the last I saw of him. What's this coming to, Johnny?'

He cleared his throat.

'It's this way, Mr. Preston — er — say, ain't it funny? This is just a matter of business, but because it's you I can't seem to get it out.'

'Very funny. Try harder,' I suggested.

He looked at me oddly.

'I feel kinda responsible for Race. We

was kinda buddies really, in a way. I don't know where this friend of his fits in, seeing I don't even know who it is. But around here, around Monkton, I sorta feel like the only surviving relative. Know what I mean?'

If he was going to turn the screw on me, he was going a long way round. I nodded.

'And?'

'I ain't too well-heeled, Mr. Preston. But things are a lot better than they were when you picked me off the floor. Fact is — well, here it is. I'd like to hire you.'

'Hire me?'

My voice sounded small. It had a right. I was feeling pretty small.

'Yeah. You may think I have a helluva nerve, and maybe you're right. But I'd like to hire you to find out who this friend was. And after that maybe we can take it on a piece.'

'You mean find out who killed him?'

I felt ashamed of what I'd been thinking. Lugio's hesitancy had been due, not to what my nasty little mind imagined, but to a reluctance to put me

61

in the position of being employed by him. Looking at his eager face now, I could have kicked myself.

'Johnny, you want to think this over,' I told him. 'I don't have a thing to go on with this friend. This is a big town we have here, with an awful lot of people. One of them knew Rendell, may be.'

'But you have ways of finding out things,' he interrupted.

'That I do,' I agreed. 'But this kind of investigation takes time. And time runs into money. A lot of money. I don't want you to bust yourself paying me.'

He waved away the argument.

'I appreciate what you're saying. Sure, I know you have to charge for your time, and I know you'll give me a square deal. But if you get a break early, and you could, maybe it won't take so long, huh?'

'Maybe. But don't count on it,' I warned.

He rubbed fingers against the evening stubble on his chin.

'That's fair, and I appreciate it. Look.'

He slid an envelope across the table.

'Don't open it in here,' he cautioned.

'Just put it straight in your pocket. There's a hundred bucks in there, Mr. Preston. You start asking your questions. When the century runs out of time, let me know how you're doing. If you're getting close, I'm in for a few more bucks. If not, we'll call it off. O.K.?'

I put the envelope in my coat. A hundred was a lot of folding money to Johnny Lugio. It was a pity Race Rendell would never know what a good friend he had.

'I'll think about it,' I promised. 'If I think we have a chance I'll keep the money. Otherwise, I'll send it back tomorrow. How does that fit?'

'Like a glove, custom-made.'

We shook hands quickly.

'Before I go, you're absolutely certain you can't remember a thing Race ever told you about this friend? Nothing ever made you suspect it was a woman he was sweet on, for example?'

'I been racking my brains. Nothing.'

'Well, if you remember anything, anything at all, let me know. Oh and Johnny — '

'Yes Mr. Preston?'

'This is between us. Strictly. And it has to stay that way.'

'You got a bet.'

I left him and went off to keep my appointment with Sam Thompson at Dino's. It was not a very long journey distance-wise, but difference-wise the two bars could have been at opposite poles. Dino's catered for the cross-town traffic and it drew cross-town people. Business guys late home, clubgoers starting early. People say if you drink long enough in Dino's, sooner or later everybody in town passes through. I once knew a man claimed he'd been propping up the mahogany bar every night for six years, and he'd still only seen half the population. That is the claim, and I merely record the fact.

One of the people undoubtedly passing through tonight was Sam Thompson. He had contrived to spread himself along the bar so generously that when he drew himself together there was space enough for me to squeeze in.

'You're late,' he grumbled.

'You can spare the extra five minutes. What happened?'

'Mr. Ventura is a hard man to follow. He double-tracked, checked, back-tracked, doubled back again. That man has been tailed before.'

It sounded like an excuse.

'So you lost him?'

Sam was offended at once.

'I didn't say he'd ever been tailed by me before,' he said huffily. 'No, I didn't lose him. He finished up in an apartment house on West 17th. The Courtenay. You know it?'

I knew it.

'It's a large building. You couldn't narrow down the address a little?'

'Wish you'd wait till I finish. He went to see a dame. Apartment 310. Name of Arabella Bell.'

I looked at him sourly.

'That has to be a gag.'

He shook his head.

'You know I never make jokes in bars. A man has his principles.'

'All right, what's with this dame? She some kind of show-biz nut?'

65

Thompson sighed.

'I guess I let you down. I follow the guy for an hour. Then in a twenty-two storey block I find out which number he wants. I even find out who rents the place. What do I get? Complaints. I'm sorry I don't know what the dame does for a living. I don't even know what kind of perfume she uses. I couldn't even tell you — '

'All right, Sam, all right. I got the message. Any more?'

'What kind of more?'

'Like did he come out again, did anybody else go in, stuff like that?'

He chewed noisily at a pretzel.

'Nope. I hung around for ten or fifteen minutes. Nobody went in or out. Then I had to come on here to meet you.'

'Fine, Sam. A little progress. Maybe I'll call you tomorrow.'

'O.K. Er — I hate to mention money — '

'No, you don't. You don't hate one single thing about money. Even the mention of it.'

I pulled out Lugio's envelope, and opened it.

'I should get that kind of mail,' said Sam.

There was a thin sheaf of bills inside. I pulled them out, and put a ten on the counter.

'That's for the feet.'

Thompson looked at it without enthusiasm, I laid another ten beside the first. He brightened.

'That's for being around to bat people at the right time.'

'Jes' fine, boss,' he cackled.

'And spare me the Mississippi dialogue. Don't blow it all on liquor. Not tonight anyway. If I need you tomorrow, you'll want to be in some kind of shape.'

'Will do.'

He nodded and ambled out. I still wasn't clear whether the last remark meant he would drink the whole twenty, or whether he'd be in shape the following day.

'It's a bar,' said a voice.

I looked up to see an unfriendly face over a white jacket.

'Huh?' I asked.

'It's a bar,' he repeated. 'People come

in here, they buy drinks, they drink 'em. It's happening all over.'

'And?'

'And if you want a place to flop, this ain't it. You buying a drink or not?'

Him I didn't like. I shook my head.

'Just looking the place over,' I told him. 'Think I'll do my drinking elsewhere.'

His face said that was all right with him, and I went out. It was a stand-off. Outside, the evening was warm and a light breeze was coming in off the ocean. It was a night to be thinking of pleasant things, even maybe doing one or two. It was no night to be going up against a character like Julian Ventura. I headed for the Courtenay Apartments.

4

West 17th Street is a coming street. Monkton City is a mixture of the old and the new. It had been a quiet little town until the advent of World War II. Then, with defense plants springing up on every waste lot in Southern California, the place grew and went on growing. Some parts of the old town became very fashionable, others went downhill fast. And all the time there was new money pouring into the city from new plants, new housing projects, every kind of human activity. We have a saying around that there are just two classifications for the streets. There are coming streets and going streets and those definitions mean exactly what you imagine. As I say, West 17th is a coming street, and that means new acres of concrete and shiny glass, new automobiles, new stores, everything new, new, new. I'm not saying whether it's good or bad, I'm just saying it is.

The Courtenay Apartments stands four-square on the site of old Jebediah Watson's stables. Jeb ran some fine horses in those days, and what with the riding academy, and renting his animals out to the movie studios, he made a fat living for himself and his three sons. Jeb Watson was a well-known and popular figure around the town, and when he died a couple of years ago, people shook their heads and said things would never be quite the same. They were right, too. His sons formed into a corporation called the Three-W Business Enterprises. First the riding academy went, then the horses. Finally the Watson boys went too, but not before they sold out their lush pastorage to a real estate company. The real-estate boys didn't know too much about horses and pasture, but they knew a choice building lot when they saw it. And now the two hundred foot man-made cliff known as the Courtenay building towers up from the ground. I sighed as I went through the massive glass doors, and wondered what Jeb would have made of it all.

The rental of the apartments was way out of the feed and grain category, and I was anxious to take a look at Arabella Bell, whoever she might be. I was less anxious for a second encounter with Ventura but you have to take the thorns with the roses. No. 310 looked harmless enough from the outside. There was no buzzer. The caller had to pass his hand over a square tag displaying the number, and musical chimes sounded inside. It is the kind of gimmick that tickles the minds of the kiddywinks, and adds another ten per month to the charges. The door opened quickly and a dishy redhead was about to say something, when she saw me and looked disappointed instead.

'Yes?'

It was a pity she was disappointed. I wasn't. She had a soft round face which stopped this side of dimples. Her attire stopped, or I should say slowed, this side of the decency regulations. There was a piece of black material about the size and shape of two coffee cups which made a pretence of covering the upper half of her

71

full lush body. And when I say coffee cups, I don't refer to the kind people use at breakfast. These would be banquet size, where they measure the coffee by spoonfuls. She also wore a pair of emerald green capris but it took me several seconds to get down that far. Her feet were bare.

'On the street you could get arrested for what you're thinking,' she told me. But I couldn't detect any note that she was offended. 'What do you want?'

'Miss Arabella Bell?'

Even though I knew I was going to say it, it still sounded ridiculous.

'What do you want?' she repeated.

'I'm from the T.V. International News,' I said smoothly. 'We are running a feature on people with interesting names. Yours is on my list. I wonder if you could spare a few moments?'

'I don't get it,' she said. But a hand strayed to her hair, which was already immaculate.

'It's just a small human interest feature,' I went on. 'Please, before we go on, don't let me give you the wrong impression. So many people immediately feel there's a chance of a great television career when we run a show of this kind. I have to be perfectly honest with you, Miss Bell. The interview probably wouldn't screen for more than fifteen seconds, maybe less, and the strong chance is it would lead absolutely nowhere. Part of my job to make that plain from the start.'

She nodded uncertainly.

'That's plain enough. But I still don't get it.'

'Perhaps if you could spare me a moment? Five minutes should be plenty.'

After one last look at my honest face she opened the door.

'I guess it's all right.'

She stood back and I went into a room that looked more like an old Hollywood set than a place where people were supposed to live.

'Sit yourself down. Can I get you a cigaret? I'm having one.'

'Thank you.'

She swayed across to a white painted cabinet. Not that I was looking at the cabinet. I was mesmerised by the tight swinging rump in the green pants. Wondering too, how a dame who looked like that could be so dumb as to let a total stranger into her apartment at night. She opened the twin doors and put her hand inside. Then she turned around. I expected her to be holding a pack of cigarets. Instead I was looking at a small nickel-plated automatic, which didn't look at all sociable.

'Don't think this is just for ornament,' she advised. I spread my hands.

'Whatever you say, Miss Bell. Could I ask what this is all about?'

She grinned, but it was not attractive. Somehow, the gun made Arabella a whole woman. She didn't look uncomfortable or awkward the way most women do with a gun. Instead, she looked as though the weapon were a part of her, an old and trusted piece of normal equipment.

'Brother,' she assured me. 'I don't know the answer to that. This is all your idea.'

I gave it one last try.

'I'm from T.V. International News,' I began patiently. 'We — '

'Leave it,' she snapped. 'I knew a guy one time worked for that outfit. It's a standing rule of the company when they call on people, they have to show identification before they start talking. Keep your hands where they are.'

My hands froze.

'I was only reaching for identification,' I said calmly.

'Too late. Even if you have some kind of phoney papers, you broke another rule. If those boys have to interview a woman who lives alone, they always send two men. Always.'

I uttered a few silent words about the stupid regulation of T.V. International News.

'I'm just an old rule-breaker, I guess.'

'No,' she contradicted. 'Right now you're just an old house-breaker. And there ain't a jury anywhere who'll find anything wrong with it if I put a hole or two in you. Defenseless girl alone in apartment late at night. You know how it'll read.'

I didn't like the way things were going.

'But I didn't know you were alone,' I

said evenly. 'I thought he'd still be here.'

'Who?' she asked sharply, the gun steady on my chest.

'Why, Julian,' I replied in a surprised tone. 'Are there others?'

She bit her lip.

'Who did you say?'

But some of the confidence was gone. In her eyes there was a new expression, of alarm or worry I couldn't be sure.

'Julian said to come here if I needed him. It's a little business thing. He probably didn't bother you with it.'

'I don't know any Julian.'

'Ventura,' I supplemented. 'At least, that's his name this week. He always lands on his feet, that guy. Swell apartment, swell looking dame. When's he coming back?'

I lounged back in the chair to show how much at ease I was. I'd have felt easier still if the gun showed any inclination to waver. But the round black hole stared with unwinking fascination at my middle.

'I don't know nobody by that name,' she assured me.

By a superhuman effort I contrived a laugh that didn't sound too hollow.

'What do you know?' I chuckled. 'He's done it again. So he isn't Ventura this week. Let's see what we have in the stock room. He was Dandy Davis one time in Fresno. No good? Er, in Denver he went by the name of Elisha Hammet. No, wait a minute, that was Vegas. In Denver it was — h'm — funny how you can't always remember names.'

But she was listening. Hard.

'Your friend has a lot of names.'

'You know how it is. Guy travels around some, he don't like to be tied down too much.'

'Yeah. He must be a very interesting man. What does he look like?'

'Joe?' Then noticing her face, 'Sorry, I didn't tell you. That's his real name, Joe. What does he look like?'

I gave her a snarl by scowl description of Ventura. She nodded.

'Maybe I do know somebody looks like that.'

'Aw, I knew that all the time. You don't take chances. That's smart. Could we put the thing away now?'

She looked down at the gun, hesitated, then lowered it.

'He'll be back later. Had to go see some people. What's it about?'

I grinned and hunched my shoulders.

'Look, you're a nice-looker and all that, but I don't think Joe'd like it if I went around telling everybody his business.'

It was the kind of talk she understood, and it made sense.

'Have it your way. You gonna wait for him?'

I consulted my watch.

'Not for too long. I have people to see myself. Any liquor around?'

That's the kind of thing I do. Everything is all set and moving the way I want it, then I gum up the whole deal. All the thaw disappeared at once and she flew to where she'd put the gun.

'That does it,' she hissed. 'You had me going there for a minute, but that puts you in a different league.'

The gun was back at the same old stand, and I sighed.

'Not that again. I thought we fixed all that?'

'Not quite,' she corrected. 'Not when you don't even know your dear good friend Joe is practically an alkie. He wouldn't stay ten minutes any place there was no bottle.'

Me and my big mouth.

'Can't win 'em all.'

'Not this one, brother. Now who are you, and what do you want?'

'How much do you know already?' I countered.

'It's my gun. I talk when it suits me. First you.'

I shrugged.

'He wants something. I know where it is.'

'What kind of something?' she demanded.

'Uh uh,' I negatived. 'No soap. He's the one wants it. Him I tell.'

She waggled the little gun.

'You're forgetting something,' she reminded.

'Arabella, I never forget anything,' I assured her. 'So far as that toy is concerned you might as well throw it out the window. He wants it. I've got it. You blow holes in me, he won't get it. And he'll get sore. You want to be the one who makes him that way. He's an awful mean man when he's upset. Put it away and let's have that drink.'

She laughed. It was a brief shrill sound.

'You don't scare easy, do you? I won't put it away, but I'll quit pointing it. You still want a drink?'

'Why not?'

'It's in there. Get me one too.'

I went to the cabinet and splashed out some scotch. There were enough bottles inside to float a distillery. She showed me the automatic again while I handed over the glass, then rested it on a cushion beside her.

'How well do you know Julian?' she demanded.

'Not at all,' I admitted. 'I just met him the one time. You don't know him very well either.'

'Skip that.' She leaned towards me and without the artillery I was forcibly reminded that this was a woman. 'Tell about the merchandise, the stuff you have.'

'It's worth a lot of money.'

'How much money?' she asked, and her eyes were greedy.

My eyes must have been getting greedy too, the way the little black cups jostled and jounced around. And what was inside wasn't coffee at all.

'Why do you want to know?'

'Just nosey.'

'Take my advice baby. Don't get nosey around Julian. He doesn't like nosey people.'

'You don't know him, you just said so,' she pointed out.

'That's right. But I know about him. I've known about him a long time. And he's very bad company when he's crossed. How'd you come to take up with him?'

'Now who's nosey?' she asked suspiciously.

'Me. I am. You're a dish, Arabella, and nobody could accuse Ventura of impersonating Rock Hudson.'

'Ah, what do you know? You know nothing. You think that's all a gal wants in this world? Let me tell you, I've been around some. Quite some. When a gal finds somebody like him, she hangs around till the train leaves.'

'Why?'

She threw back her head and sighed. The coffee cups did a little dance. Any other time she could have had me dancing too.

'The man's a spender. He looks after me good. All I have to do is not bother him when he's drinking, and see he has a good time when he's sober. Soft deal.'

'And not ask any questions,' I added.

She looked across with derision.

'Where they been hiding you, boy? A gal who asks a man questions deserves what she gets. I don't rock any boats. This'll really bring in some gravy, this stuff you have?'

'I don't really have it,' I pointed out. 'I just know where it is. And before I tell your big brother, I have to be sure he can pay.'

'Pay how much?' she asked quickly.

I wagged an admonitory finger.

'There you go again. Let's just say, plenty. You been with him long?'

82

' 'Bout a week. Hey, what's that to you?'

'Nothing.'

I stood up. At once she grabbed up her best friend and put it where I couldn't miss it. And vice versa.

'It's been nice Arabella, but I have to go now.'

'Stay right where you are.'

I turned my back on her.

'You're crazy,' she said, in a frightened tone.

'Not really. This way, if you squeeze that thing, I get it in the back. You might swing a lot of juries in that outfit. But not when the holes are in my back. Tell him I'll be back tomorrow.'

I couldn't see what she was doing behind me, which was probably a good thing for my peace of mind. But I walked to the door and opened it. The whole of my back was prickly with fear. I stepped out and swung the door shut. As I put space between me and Apartment 310 I felt myself loosening up. By the time I got back to the Chev I was normal. When I went to West 17th I'd intended to see

83

Ventura. Arabella Bell had changed my mind, and put some new ideas in there.

It was almost eleven o'clock when I got to Parkside Towers. Enough is enough as the man says, and I planned on nothing more strenuous than the late night movie and a quiet drink. I let myself into the apartment and snapped down the switch.

Then I just stood looking.

5

Someone must have annoyed a tribe of apes and then turned them loose in the apartment. Nothing else could have caused so much mess. Everything that could be emptied was empty. Everything rippable was ripped. Cushions had been slit open, drawers overturned, the whole place was a nightmare.

My first thought was that my friends might still be waiting around with a little surprise for me. Quietly, I closed the door and slipped the .38 into my hand. Now I felt better. Prowling around like a burglar, I poked my head in every conceivable hiding place. Nothing. Reassured at least on that point, I put away the hardware and poured myself a drink. Not the intended beer either, but a good slug of scotch. Somebody up here didn't like me. Or didn't like me having something. No prizes were offered for guessing what that something might be. I was glad to note no amateurs had been employed. No possible hiding place for the yellow oilskin had been missed, for one thing. For another, they hadn't gone crazy when they realised the stuff wasn't there. Amateurs do. Amateurs and second-raters destroy things with no purpose, sometimes start a fire. Not these boys. There was method and precision in the way they'd reduced the place to a garbage dump.

One thing we boast at Parkside is round the clock service. I rang down for the night man, and he came up a couple of minutes later. I let him in.

'Oh, it's you, Frank. Thought you were on days.'

'No, Mr. Preston. Charlie's wife is sick and — holy mackerel. What did you do? Have a fit?'

'Almost, when I first saw it,' I admitted.

He looked around in wonder.

'Did you see anybody unusual?' I asked.

'No.' He scratched his head. 'No, not that I recall. Kinda busy tonight though. Any valuables missing, Mr. Preston?'

'Nothing, so far as I can see.'

'Nuts, huh? I've heard of 'em pulling this kind of stuff before. Not here, though. Not at the Towers. Company ain't gonna like this.'

'Why do we have to tell the company?' I queried.

'Can't hardly help it, can we? The papers'll find out from the police, and it ain't gonna be what you call a real secret then, is it?'

I took out Lugio's envelope and extracted some bills.

'Frank, I wouldn't upset the company for the world. Now why don't you take this and chew on it a while. Then tomorrow morning, after I clear out, you get some buddy of yours in here, and make the place look like home again.'

He looked at the money and liked it. But the idea wasn't so attractive.

'Gee, I don't know Mr. Preston. This here's a crime, and the police wouldn't like it if nobody told 'em.'

'That's not quite right. It isn't a crime until it's reported,' I corrected. Incorrectly. 'All it is right now is a mess. And

I'd like it cleaned up.'

'No police, huh?'

'No police.'

He stuck the money in his pocket and grinned.

'Well, long as nobody got hurt I guess it's all right. About ten in the morning?'

'Ten will be fine.'

He went out. I wandered disconsolately around picking up things and putting them down somewhere else. I wasn't making any noticeable improvement, so I went to bed.

★ ★ ★

Next morning I was out of the apartment by nine thirty and on my way to the office. Florence Digby was already in position, cool calm and orderly.

'There was a call a few minutes ago,' she announced. 'They asked for you to call back.'

'Who was it at this hour?' I grumbled.

'Delaney, Parker and Smith.'

She said it slowly, and with careful articulation so I didn't miss the message.

I heard her all right.

'Delaney, Par — are you sure?'

'If you'd like me to check the number with the supervisor — ' she began coldly.

'No. Naturally not.'

Delaney and his partners were one of the most influential firms of lawyers in the city. No crime business for them. They dealt in solid gilt-edge like real-estate, company business and so forth. I've been around a while but I never had any business from those guys, not yet anyway.

'What's it all about, did they say?'

'Mercy, no. I spoke personally with Mr. Delaney's secretary. That's young Mr. Delaney of course, the son.'

'The old one would be the father, huh?'

'Yes, he — '

She stopped, biting her lip. I oughtn't to poke fun at Florence that way, but she has this bug about the big business operations, and the old families and stuff like that. Once she starts rattling on, you're liable to wind up with a kind of short version of a Monkton City Who's Who and Business Directory, if you don't put a stop to it.

'And what did this personal gal say?'

'She simply said Mr. Delaney would like to speak with you, and if you were not available, perhaps you could call back when you were free. I'll get the number.'

'Whoa,' I said. 'I'm not free yet. I'll let you know.'

'But Mr. Preston,' she protested. 'I'm speaking of Mr. Delaney of Delaney, Parker and Smith.'

'Bully for you. And you're speaking to Mr. Preston, of Preston Investigations and Breakfast. Which I haven't yet had. Be back in half an hour.'

She was so furious she could think of nothing else to say as I went out. There's a little Italian place close by, and there I took aboard some ham and waffles, and half a bucket of coffee. While I was eating I sifted over the meager information I'd gleaned, and it didn't tell me much. It looked as though I'd have to apply Method One of my Course for Student Operators. The first essential to an investigation is the positive knowledge that there is something going on. Then it helps if you have some idea as to the nature of the something. Once you know that, the chances are you will know some names, and some of those names may belong to people who know more than you. After that it's plain sailing, relatively speaking. All you do is to go around making a lot of noise, maybe bragging some, and sooner or later someone is going to worry about you. The worried one will then want to do something about you, or to you, and this way things begin to come out in the open. That's Method One. I like to call it Method One because it impresses the freshmen. But the plain truth is, I never had any other method.

At the moment, all I had was Ventura. I'd made some noises at him in my own office. Then I'd been to Arabella's apartment and made more noises, just to let Julian know I was aware of his address. The next move would be his, and he was certain to make one, if only because I'd lifted his roll. Somehow I didn't figure him for the turning over of my apartment. I hadn't any facts to support the feeling, but if it was right, then there were others taking more than a passing interest in me. I hadn't the remotest idea as to who or what they might be, so I couldn't make noises in their direction. The telephone call from Clifford Delaney was another thing I couldn't figure. But one thing was certain, there could be no connection between that particular firm and murder. Delaney and his partners were not to be confused with any sidestreet shysters. They were four-square pillars of respectability, and none of them would sleep for weeks at any suggestion of a connection with racetrack characters who bled to death in parking lots. So I was more than mildly curious when I strolled back to the office and asked Miss Digby to get them on the phone. She managed to ice her way through the outer defenses but she couldn't get access to the great man. Regretfully, she switched me through. The inner defense consisted of Mr. Delaney's personal secretary, who wouldn't even tell me her name.

'Oh yes, Mr. Preston. Mr. Delaney would like you to call and see him as soon as possible.'

Where I come from we don't take messages.

'Fine,' I replied. 'Put Mr. Delaney on, will you?'

'That won't be necessary,' she told me sweetly, 'He's only going to ask you the same thing.'

'Have it your way. Tell Delaney, when he wants me, he can call me up. You already have the number.'

I put the phone down before she could argue. I broke out a new pack of Old Favorites and stripped off the foil. I was into my second puff when the bell jangled. A man said:

'Preston, is that you? What is all this foolishness? Oh, my name is Delaney.'

'What foolishness were you talking about?' I asked.

'This nonsense of refusing to speak with my secretary. She was only trying — '

'She was only trying to save your valuable time,' I finished. 'Well, when people want me, they want me. They're not usually too busy to tell me so in person. And I notice you're calling me now.'

There was a spluttering noise as though he had trouble with his teeth.

'All right. Let's leave the subject. Now then, will you or will you not come here to see me?'

'What about?'

'About a matter which will interest you, and which I cannot discuss other than face to face.'

'I see. If it isn't going to take too long, I can be there in twenty minutes.'

'Thank you,' he said heavily, as though the words had been torn from his throat. 'Twenty minutes.'

Having struck this insignificant blow for the democratic principle, I went out to Miss Digby.

'Going to see Delaney. May not get back till the afternoon.'

She nodded abstractedly as though it were of no importance. And of course, it wasn't. Florence Digby runs the thing anyhow. I often think she could do it entirely alone, except she could hardly be expected to take the lumps as well. That was my featured role. Lumps man. Delaney, Parker and Smith occupied the two top floors of an old five storey building that had been the nearest thing to a skyscraper fifty years ago. Many of the other old buildings on that street have gone, long replaced by towering boxes that dwarf the Delaney building and one or two others like it. Instead of being old-fashioned and years behind the times, it was getting to be the hip thing to get office space in one of the old buildings. They've been there a long time, and they give you the feeling the occupants have been there a long time too. Which is very good for inspiring confidence in the customers. Not that Delaney etc., etc., needed any gimmicks in that direction. Old Henry Delaney had been a railroad lawyer. He came to Monkton at the turn of the century to negotiate with some local landowners for a right of way for the new railroad. Henry and Monkton City took one look at each other and it was bye-bye railroad. He hung up his shingle, enrolled the landowners as his first clients, and drove a hard bargain with his former employers. Monkton was primarily a farming community those days, and the coming of the railroad was just the boost the town needed. The place grew and prospered, and of course in that mysterious way of things, the man who got most of the credit was Henry Delaney. He became so much a part of the town, that when he died they closed down all the stores. Everybody turned out that day, to pay their respects to one of the last giants of the freebooting tycoon era. And to watch the sorrowing widow and her family. Too often, when a big man goes, the offspring soon show themselves to be several notches lower on the achievement scale. But old Henry's boys did him proud. There were two of them, one now dead, and the other virtually retired from active business. That was Henry Delaney II, the elder son, and very much like his father. I would have enjoyed meeting Henry, but I was going to have to be content with his son Clifford.

I walked up the elaborate staircase to the third floor. Up here it was plain there was no room for the ideas of a modern architect. There weren't any clean functional lines or space saving tricks. But there was an atmosphere of comfort and quiet. The receptionist followed the general trend. She was comfortable, several sizes comfortable, and quiet with it.

'I said Mr. Delaney's expecting me,' I repeated.

She smiled warmly and most of her chins joined in.

'What name shall I say?' she asked, in not much above a whisper.

I told her and she made sibilant noises into a telephone.

'Miss Stella will be right out.'

I had just the one chin, but I gave it all I had as I smiled my thanks. Miss Stella came through a door at the far end, and Mr. Delaney didn't seem so important any more. She had a froth of blonde hair and an oval face with good features and sparkling teeth. She wore a severe green blouse tucked into a crisp white skirt, and neither of them were kidding anybody there wasn't a lot of woman inside.

'Mr. Preston?'

Somebody ought to have told Miss Stella about the smile routine. Not only did she forget to crack her face, but her voice sounded like chips of ice dropping into a champagne bucket.

'Yes. Miss Stella?' I returned.

She ignored that.

'Mr. Delaney will see you at once. If you will come this way, please.'

I would come this way please. I would go any way she said, just so I could walk to one side of her and slightly behind, looking down on the blonde curls and drinking in perfume. The walk to Mr. Delaney's office seemed unnecessarily short. She turned and looked at me. I wagged my tail but she was no animal lover.

'Will you wait please?'

I waited while she tapped on a solid looking door and slipped inside. Almost at once it was opened again and she held it wide.

'Mr. Preston, Mr. Delaney.'

Then she was gone and I was marching across acres of plush carpeting towards a man who rose from behind an all-glass desk. He was probably forty years old, under six feet tall, with the build of a former athlete. The crew cut hair was graying at the sides, and all in all you could take it the women would not run screaming from Mr. Delaney. He stuck out a hand and we shook briefly.

'Sit down, won't you? Cigaret?'

I sat down as he slid a piece of the glass desk top sideways. There was a cavity filled with Old Favorites, and I nodded with approval as I took one.

'My own brand, Mr. Delaney. Very thoughtful.'

He laughed pleasantly.

'A coincidence, I fear. My father would never smoke anything else, and its become a part of the office routine.'

I knew I'd have got along with Henry.

'That's a fine desk, if you don't mind my saying so,' I commented.

He was really pleased this time.

'Isn't it? It's my worst extravagance since I more or less took control from my father. It's claimed to be an exact replica of one in Mussolini's home. Whether that's true or not, I can't say. I'd have bought it anyway.'

I exhaled smoke, which was promptly

trapped by an eddy of breeze and whisked towards the air-conditioning plant.

'Are you an admirer of Mussolini, Mr. Delaney?' I asked casually.

He stared at me coolly across the shining glass.

'That's twice within an hour you've been, shall we say, provocative? Are you out to pick a fight with me? And if so, why?'

'Not specially. And I don't have a reason. Mussolini's gang killed an uncle of mine back there in the thirties. I wouldn't want to do any business with his friends.'

'I see. Well, you may rest your conscience. I detest the mention of the man. That isn't any reason I shouldn't buy a desk if I like it.'

He made it a statement and looked to see if I had any further bids. I hadn't.

'I don't believe we have had any dealings with your firm before?'

He knew damn well we hadn't, and he knew I knew it, but I'd had my quota of sour remarks for a spell.

'That's right,' I nodded.

'Nevertheless, you are known to us by reputation.'

I dipped ash into a silver tray mounted on a heavy ebony stand.

'You said that without inflection, Mr. Delaney,' I pointed out. 'It would help me a little if you could elaborate on it.'

He gave me a quick searching glance to see whether I was ribbing him again. I wasn't.

'Very well. Our information is that you are honest and reliable. You are unusually independent, and not famous for your tact. You are also a little bit tough, but I imagine that is a prerequisite of success in your — ah — line of endeavour. Is that enough?'

'More than enough,' I assured him.

'Good. Then let us proceed. One of our clients is in need of your services. There is a housing project out at West Shore which I have no doubt you'll have passed by at some time.'

'I know it. Big project. One of these F.O.L. Construction deals isn't it? Nothing but the biggest?'

'Correct. In fact, our client is that same

company. The work is getting behind schedule. The reason is that someone is deliberately sabotaging. Equipment gets mysteriously damaged, materials stolen. Last week some blast charges were set off during the night, and the damage is estimated at thirty thousand dollars.'

'Whow. Labor troubles?'

'No.' He set his hands on the glass desk and the reflection seemed to be a spare set of fingers growing underneath. 'No, that is the extraordinary feature of this business. Ordinarily, I would have expected just what you suggest. But the labor force is extremely well content. The company pay well above the Union minimum, and there are progressive bonuses and so forth. In fact, I may tell you in confidence, the union have themselves approached the company, because of course with all these delays, deadlines are falling behind.'

'And bonuses are not being paid,' I murmured.

'Precisely.'

'How about another company?' I suggested.

Delaney raised his eyebrows.

'Are you serious?'

'Perfectly. If F.O.L. don't keep to their datelines, maybe they lose a big contract and somebody else is anxious to pick it up.'

His eyes gleamed.

'Ah, I see. Yes, a very ingenious suggestion. Not applicable in this instance, because the project is wholly self-financed.'

'All right, I give up,' I admitted. 'What's your theory?'

'A madman. Probably actually working on the project himself. I can think of nothing else.'

I ground out my Old Favorite.

'You could be right, I guess. But where do I fit in all this?'

He leaned across the desk towards me.

'We'd like you to take a job there. Regular employment. This would give you an opportunity to get to know the men. You could keep your eyes open and see what happened.'

'Whoa.' I held up a hand. 'Mr. Delaney, those guys would know I was a phoney right off. I don't know from first base about building anything.'

'There's a site office. You would be fitted in there. The duties are simple routine. No-one would suspect you of being other than an ordinary employee like themselves.'

'I'd have to think about it,' I hedged. 'I have other work on hand. This thing would take up about ten hours a day. There wouldn't be time for anything else.'

'Eleven,' he corrected. 'But you wouldn't need any other work. The company will pay you one fifty a day. With one day's notice either way.'

Right then a tiny voice began to trill in the back of my head. It was too much money. Trying to sound casual I said:

'It's an awful lot of money, Mr. Delaney. Are things that bad?'

His eyes widened appreciatively.

'That's very frank of you. I agree, it is a lot of money. In fact, I'll return your frankness. I advised my client against exceeding fifty dollars a day and expenses. I would have considered that more than adequate. However, the decision did not rest with me. I am simply passing on my client's instructions.'

I was glad he'd said it. It made him sound more like a descendant of Henry I and Henry II.

'I'm not denying it's a good offer,' I told him. 'Maybe in a couple of days I'll be able to take you up on it. Right now, I have things to finish.'

Now he didn't understand.

'Other things?' he muttered vaguely. 'Surely with an offer of this kind — ?'

He let it hang in the air. I looked up and saw the rest of the sentence. What he left unsaid was that with an offer of that kind a man could afford to drop everything.

'Look Mr. Delaney, I don't know how you and Parker and Smith run your business. The way I run mine, somebody gives me a job to do, I do it. I don't just walk out on them every time somebody else waves a buck under my nose. Like I said, I hope to wind up this other thing in a day or two. If the offer is still open then, I'll think about it.'

'You couldn't possibly turn over your

other — oh — investigation to someone else? That way you could make everybody happy.'

It sounded a sensible solution. No doubt it was, from where Delaney was sitting. But not from my chair.

'Mr. Delaney,' I explained patiently. 'There are some people around just at this time who don't like me. They are liable to translate this feeling into more positive form any minute now. Unless I beat them to it. So you see, it wouldn't be any use my trying to swing this on someone else. It's me those people want, not a substitute.'

He nodded.

'Very well. I can't of course guarantee that my clients will not make alternative arrangements meantime.'

'That's understood.'

I got up to leave.

'Oh by the way, I don't mind talking to your secretary next time. Not now I've seen her. Who should I ask for?'

He chuckled then.

'You really are an odd character. Her name is Delaney.'

'Oh,' I said disappointedly. 'That wouldn't be maybe your wife out there?'

'Heaven forbid,' he replied. 'The lady is my sister. And Preston — '

He leaned forward confidentially, checking to be sure the intercom was switched off.

' — If you think you can handle some real trouble, try my secretary.'

It was a compliment. He wasn't a man who went around offering to sell his sister. He was talking to me as an equal, and from a Monkton City Delaney that's a lot of compliment.

'Thanks for the tip. I'll call you.'

I went out. The delectable Stella was writing something with a gold pen in a leather-covered book. She didn't look up.

'You always get sore so easily?' I queried.

The pen stopped moving and she looked up at me with glinting eyes.

'If you've finished your business with Mr. Delaney, the way out is through that door.'

I grinned.

'Somebody once told me you were a

bad-tempered hussy. I can see what he meant.'

It isn't easy to ignore somebody when they make a provocative remark like that. Especially if you're a female.

'How dare you speak to me like that?' she demanded.

'Why not? What makes you so special?'

'Why, you, you ill-mannered lout,' she spluttered.

'Don't worry, I'm going. You must be a pretty bad stenographer, huh?'

She gave a heavy artificial sigh and laid the pen on the desk. Then she folded her arms and looked at me with loathing.

'All right, if it's the only way to get rid of you. Why must I be a bad stenographer?'

'It's obvious. Nobody with any sense works with relatives unless they have to. You don't have to. That makes it look as though your family are the only people who'll give you a job, doesn't it?'

'I'll have you know that at business college, I was the — oh, why do I bother to explain to you. You know where the door is. And I'm busy.'

'You mean you'd explain it if you weren't busy?' I asked.

'I might. What are you doing?'

I flicked down the key on the inter-office talk-box.

'Yes?'

Delaney's voice crackled through.

'Mr. Delaney, your sister says she'd like to come out with me for some coffee, if you could spare her for ten minutes.'

'Is that you, Preston?'

'It is.'

He chuckled, and Stella Delaney's face was furious.

'Take all the time you need.'

'Thanks.'

I switched off.

'What sort of adolescent trick is this?' she demanded.

'Now, now,' I wagged a finger. 'I only took you up on what you said. Of course, if you're a bad loser — '

'No.' She stood up. 'I'll come, if only to find out whether you're as awful as you seem.'

6

I took her to Hoffers which is on the same block as the office, and has a reputation for coffee among other things. We sat down at a window table covered with a red check cloth.

'Why'd you come?' I asked her.

'I've been wondering the same thing. I'm not exactly desperate for coffee. Why did you ask me?'

They came with the coffee then, tall steaming beakers with a pattern of snowy mountains and ski-slopes. The atmosphere was great, so long as you didn't look through the window at the baking pavements.

'If you were sitting here, you wouldn't need to ask that,' I told her. 'Besides, I don't like people ignoring me.'

'If it's your habit to be as rude always as you were to me, you must be used to being ignored by now.'

She stirred sugar into the mug. There

was no aggression now, and I liked her better without it.

'This could be one of those the chicken and the egg conversations,' I said.

'You know, I only get mad when people ignore me, they ignore me when I'm mad. Where does it end?'

'Tell me about this job you're going to do for Cliff,' she sidestepped.

'Not for him. For F.O.L. Construction.'

'All right. Tell me about it.'

'I'm not going to do it.'

She put her spoon back in the saucer and sipped coffee. It was hot.

'Whyever not? I would have thought it was worth while.'

'Oh, it is. But I'm busy on something else just now. Who suggested me, by the way? Somebody in the firm?'

She shook her head.

'No. Your name came from the company. They knew all about you, and they were most insistent you were the man for the job.'

'That's too bad. They'll have to get another boy this time.'

'What's it like?'

111

'Too hot.' I put down the coffee cup to emphasise the point.

'Not that. Your job. Being a private detective. All I know about it is what I see on the movies and television. I imagine it's slightly different from that.'

'Slightly. And most of it is very boring. We only have ten minutes, and I don't want to waste it by boring you. Let's have some facts.'

'Facts?'

'Facts. They're my stock-in-trade. You don't wear an engagement ring. Does that mean you're not engaged?'

'It does.'

'Fine, fine. Do you like sea food?'

'Where is all this getting us?'

I ignored the interruptions.

'About the sea food?'

'Yes, I like it fine.'

'Just two more facts and we'll be through. One, what time tonight will you be ready to eat sea food with me? Two, I'd better have your telephone number.'

She laughed then. It was the first time I'd heard it, and it had a clear, musical quality.

'Too fast, Mr. Preston. One, I have a dinner engagement tonight. Two, the office number will always find me.'

'But only in office hours,' I pointed out.

'True.' She looked at the slim platinum watch on her wrist. 'Of which I have already wasted almost twelve minutes. Thank you for coffee. If we ever meet again, try to remember I like you a lot better when you're being polite.'

And she was away, the tight white skirt moving rhythmically towards the door. It would have been a good opportunity to rifle the till. Every eye in the place was glued to that provocative rump.

'You didn't drink your coffee.'

I looked up at the thin woman who attended table.

'Er, no. Good coffee though. Just have another appointment.'

When I got outside she'd already been swallowed up by the early lunch crowd. I strolled two blocks west to Harvey Mason's office. Harve is something called a business counsellor, whatever that might be. He was busy on the phone but he grinned and waved me to a chair.

'It'll drop eight this afternoon, my personal guarantee. Huh? Swell. We'll see how Cleveland like that, O.K.? O.K.'

He broke the connection and had a look at me.

'I'm always glad to see you Preston, but tell me something. What are you doing around this way, where people do an honest day's work?'

His desk was piled high with all kinds of newspapers. I pointed.

'That's work?'

'To me it is,' he confirmed. 'A man who knows how to read the papers can make a comfortable living without stirring out of the house. When he gets real good at it, he can afford an office, too. Observe, one office.'

'Good. I'm glad you're good at it, because that's why I'm here. Will you counsel me a little business?'

'That's what it says on the sign,' he reminded.

'Let's imagine there's this old lady. All she has in the world are five hundred dollars — . No?'

I broke off because he was shaking his head sadly.

'No. Two out of three of my clients start off that way. It's never their money, they're always asking on behalf of a friend. Mostly the friend is a sweet old lady. That's so's I know from the start I'm robbing somebody's mother if I don't come good. But not from you.'

I grinned.

'I only said let's suppose. All right, if you're drinking it straight today, what's with F.O.L. Construction?'

He made a whistling noise, and sat back looking surprised.

'Well, well. Maybe you are some kind of detective at that. How'd you get on to this?'

I made deprecating noises.

'Harve, I'll tell you, I'm not on to anything. Something's come up, and it makes me want to know about F.O.L. I know they've been in business around here best part of twenty years. I never heard anything bad about them, but I want to know how they stand.'

'You've never shown any interest in the

market before,' he hedged. He didn't want to talk to me, and that was strange. I'd been a great help to Mason one time, and he wasn't the kind to forget things like that.

'I'm not interested in the market now,' I replied. 'All I want to know is anything you can give me on one particular company. What are you stalling for?'

'I'm sorry. But that one came right across the plate. I know I owe you, and I'm not losing sight of that. But a wrong word about now could lose me a lot of money, Preston. More than I can stand. I don't like to have to do this, but will you give me your word you won't repeat what I'm going to tell you?'

'You can have it so long as it isn't a confession of murder,' I told him.

He rubbed his hands in a quick, nervous gesture.

'That isn't as way out as it sounds. Oh, don't worry, I'm not talking about that kind of murder. But a killing, market wise. I am about to make one, and you can cause me grief if you spill.'

'We've been all through that. Let's have it.'

I knew what I was asking. A clam has things to learn from these share operators when it comes to handing out information. With something good about to break it was completely alien to Mason's whole scheme of things to ask him to talk about it.

'My wife always says I'm crazy,' he muttered. 'Right now, I'm beginning to agree with her. All right, here it is. F.O.L. have put every last nickel into this scheme over at West Shore. They've had to beg borrow and steal all the loose change for miles around to keep it afloat.'

'But it's a solid operation, surely? Everybody will get their money back?'

'Normally, yes. It was a good idea, the whole thing has been well planned from the start. Ordinarily, an investor could expect to collect approximately forty five percent profit inside two years. A nice piece of business by any standards.'

'What's going wrong with it?'

'You know how these things operate. At each stage of the development you have to be ready with another truckload of the green stuff, for labor and materials and so forth. I'm talking about big money now, and if you've seen the project you'll have some idea what I'm talking about.'

'I'm with you so far. But this is the normal deal, surely? People like that are always operating on credit for long periods.'

He nodded.

'It's normal. When it starts to pinch is when people begin to wonder whether the company is able to follow through. That's when they start howling about what they're owed. Others join in. The company pays out the first few to keep the noise down. Then they run out of cash. If there's still a noise going on, they try to borrow more. Only this time it's no sale around the pawnshops. That's when the whole thing disintegrates.'

'I get it. People who would usually wait for their money suddenly draw off the company capital. That leaves them broke. They can't borrow any more, and at the same time they haven't got any left to pay the men or for the next consignment of raw materials.'

'Yup,' he confirmed. 'That's how it works. And all the resources they put into the project, whatever it is, they're not worth two cents. Who needs half a bridge, or a dam with no concrete in it? Or in this case, half a ghost town? And once the confidence shows the first sign of wobbling, it'd take a minor miracle to prevent chaos.'

'And you have detected a slight wobble.'

I wasn't asking a question. It was a statement of fact. He nodded.

'You know what F.O.L. stands for, I imagine? Francis O. Lishman. He's the boss man, only very much the boss man. He built the outfit up from the ground, and he retains the strictest personal control.'

'I've heard of him,' I agreed. 'Pretty good man, they tell me.'

'The best. The West Shore development is his own personal baby. He O.K.'s every nut and bolt that goes into the place. He always works that way on the big ones, and he's made all his investors a nice piece of change every time. He's kind of arrogant with it, but nobody minds just so he's producing those results. Without him, a lot of that confidence will melt away. He's by way of being a one man genius on that kind of work.'

'Is he sick or something?' I asked innocently.

Mason laughed a denial.

'Lord, no. You wouldn't need me to give you inside information if anything like that happened. It would make the front page of every paper in town. No, it's nothing that simple. He has some new friends, that's all.'

'And that's enough to make you buy shares?'

He grinned with despair.

'Not buy Preston, sell,' he explained. 'I'm selling F.O.L.'

'I see,' I said wisely. I didn't. 'What about these friends?'

'First, think of Lishman. He's a worker. Twelve hours a day man. In his spare time he likes to play bridge. Plays all the time with old Doc Lee and that bunch.

One of the toughest games in town, all experts. He still hits a tennis ball around like a man ten years younger. Lishman is forty-seven by the way. He doesn't have a lot of time for the gals, although his wife died eight years ago. Now and then he goes out on a bender, but who doesn't? It's therapeutic. He has a few real friends, all top of some tree or other. He also has about five thousand acquaintances. Everybody says he's a great guy.'

'Got it,' I noted. 'Lishman is O.K.'

'Never doubt it. Now suddenly, a week or two back, he gets himself some new people to play with. Bad people.'

'How bad?'

'King Ralfini for one. Lucky Hertz. One or two of their business colleagues.'

He looked to see how I would take the news. I didn't like it. The King called himself a gambler, and true enough he gambled a lot. Dice, ponies, cards, everything was the same to the King. He always seemed to have a lot of money to spend, so it was a cinch he didn't lose all the time. There were some unkind people around and about who thought the King had his finger in other pies, but nobody really knew. Take his bodyguard, for example. Slats Hooper was his name, a thin myopic streak of misery with two manslaughter raps behind him. All right, maybe a gambler does need a bodyguard, but does it have to be somebody with quite such an itchy trigger finger as Slats? People thought it wasn't necessary. I was one of the people. Then there was the King's curious relationship with Lucky Hertz. Lucky ran a string of bookie joints and carried his own protection. Such a man was strange company for a gambler with a hoodlum shadow, and yet they were often together. King Ralfini with his fat happy face and gold teeth, and the quiet Hertz, slimmer built and more dapper. An ill-assorted pair physically. A lot of folks around town were very curious to know what it was brought them together, and kept them that way. But nobody was going to ask, because that would be to draw attention to their nosiness, and this was widely acknowledged to be an unwise thing to do.

'You said Lishman plays with these

birds. Would you mean that literally? I mean, does he play cards with them?'

'He does. And not bridge either. Even if he let 'em all cheat, there's not one of that bunch could hold a candle to him at bridge. Last time I heard, it was poker. And Lishman was losing.'

It seemed to me Harvey Mason was making an awful lot out of very little.

'Harve, I know you know your business. But to me this whole thing is slightly light headed. So a man plays a few hands of cards with some disreputable citizens. It's hardly justification for the collapse of a fourteen million dollar enterprise. You're sure you don't read too much into this?'

He hunched his shoulders in an extravagant shrug.

'Could be. I can't be right all the time. Of course, I can't be wrong all the time either, or I wouldn't be here. I get all the information I can. I sift it, push it into patterns, break 'em up, make new ones. Then I make what I humorously call a reasoned judgment. Said judgment, knowing the company, and the principal actors in our sordid melo-drama, tells me to sell F.O.L. Hey, that's not bad huh? Sell, like hell, F.O.L. Kinda catchy.'

I grimaced.

'Kinda creepy too. And on this hunch, sorry, reasoned judgment, you are actually spending your own money?'

'Nothing but the best,' he agreed. 'And lots of it. Come pay day, I'll have lots of lovely more.'

'You hope.'

'Amen.'

I offered cigarets but he refused.

'Why do you suppose Lishman should take up with those characters?' I asked.

'That's the big one, and I don't know the answer. I don't want to know it yet. If I'm right, the day that gets out, the market will take a severe dip. And who will be waiting around to play Santa Claus and buy those old shares at one cent apiece. None other than old Santa Mason.'

I was glad I didn't have any market dealings. Every time I bumped across it, I always came out with the feeling a private

124

richard looks wholesome by comparison.

'You say he hasn't a wife. Any other family?'

'Oh but yes, one dishy daughter. A peacheroo, I may say.'

'How about her? Could she maybe have got herself tangled up with the King or Hertz? Plenty of daddies find themselves in strange company when they meet their daughter's friends.'

Looking like a wise old owl, he wagged his head from side to side.

'A very profound observation, but it won't do, not this time. Betsy Lishman is all tooken up with a nice young guy by the name of Maurice Parker. You know the firm, Delaney, Parker and Smith.'

'Sure, I know them. I thought Parker would be an older man.'

'So he is, the one who gets his name on the letter heads. Maurice is his nephew, been with the firm a couple of years. Oh no, Lishman doesn't have to worry about his daughter. According to everybody around, those two are so stuck on each other it's embarrassing to be with them. They're getting married soon, anyhow.'

I fanned smoke through my nostrils and watched it swirl in the bright sunlight.

'Anything else you can tell me that might help?'

'What do you want? I've already jeopardised my life savings. There's nothing else to know. Besides, you didn't say why you wanted the help,' he added craftily.

'Didn't I? I'm writing a new financial column for the Globe. Have to fill it up with something.'

'Nobody should be permitted to make lousy jokes like that. They make me feel terrible.'

Joke or no, the mere thought of the publicity had wiped all the good humour off his face.

'Take it easy, Harve. The first edition isn't due till next year. And thanks for telling me — I appreciate it.'

I had plenty to think about as I went back to the office.

7

I wanted information concerning the racing fraternity, and whenever I want that, or information about almost anything else, I know where to go, I look for a walking information center who goes by the name of Charlie Surprise. I don't have to tell you that name is a phoney. Once, a long time ago, he had a much longer name. I've heard different attempts at it, like Suprosetti, Sarsparello and so forth. Anyway, people got so fed up trying to work out such a big name for such a small operator, they settled for Surprise, and it's been that way ever since. Peddling information is just a sideline with Charlie. His full-time occupation is playing the horses, and that activity needs feeding with any spare change Charlie can lay his hands on. Because he is not the same kind of horse-player as King Ralfini. He doesn't make a fat living at it. He doesn't make any kind of living at all.

Mostly, he is in to the bookies for various sums, and his life consists of finding enough winners to square himself with those impatient people before they feel it necessary to take their money's worth out of Charlie's hide.

At this time of day, Charlie would almost certainly be at the Dutchman's. I parked outside and left the bright clean sunlight behind as I stepped into the smokey dimness of the interior. There was Charlie, hunched up against the wall close by the telephone. To Charlie, the telephone plays the same part in his life that an oxygen tent does to less fortunate people. He was sucking at an inch-long pencil and peering at a much-folded newspaper.

'Got a minute, Charlie?'

He looked up with guilty apprehension, saw who it was and relaxed.

'Ain't I got troubles enough?'

I tucked a five dollar bill in the pocket of his soiled shirt.

'What's that for?'

The voice was heavy with suspicion but he didn't attempt to hand the money back.

'That's for openers,' I said quietly. 'There's going to be more.'

He shifted uneasily against the wall.

'If it's about the guy got rubbed out over at Palmtrees, I don't know nothin' about it. You want your dough back?'

I grinned reassuringly.

'Charlie, you know I wouldn't walk up to you in front of a crowd of people if I wanted that kind of stuff. This is routine information I want. And there's ten now, plus another ten if I need a little more later.'

He took the pencil from his mouth and it left a purple line on his lower lip.

'Would that be ten more than the five, or just one more five?'

'Ten more. All in all, I'm offering a quarter of a century. And you can do with it right now.'

He was suspicious again.

'What makes you say that?'

'Word gets around Charlie, it gets around. Way I've heard it, you are a man in need of twenty-five bucks.'

I didn't mention I had no idea of his present standing with the bookies. Or, I should say, no specific details of his current troubles. Because Charlie's standing, as I said earlier, seldom varies. He's always in dutch.

'Keppler's got no right to go shouting it around,' he grumbled. 'He knows I'm good for it. I never let him down yet.'

'Nobody lets Jule Keppler down,' I reminded him. 'It can be unhealthy.'

Charlie rolled his eyes and shuddered.

'Quit talking like that, Preston. You ain't a very cheerful guy, are you? Talk some more about the money.'

I looked around. There was nobody near enough to hear if we kept our voices down.

'King Ralfini,' I said very softly.

He rolled his eyes again to show the first time was no fluke.

'Goodbye. I'll give you back the five.'

I stayed put, poking at his bony chest with a forefinger.

'Is it that bad?'

'Listen, I don't know how bad. I don't want to know. I hear things. Things that tell me the King don't like guys who stick their nose in his business. That's all I need to know, brother. I'll take my chances with Jule.'

He wasn't really afraid. Not in a particular way. It was just what he regarded as natural commonsense caution to keep away from people like Ralfini.

'I'll skip the questions,' I decided. 'Just tell me about what you hear that makes the man unhealthy to talk about. I thought he was just a big time gambler.'

'Sure. With a big time hoodlum in his pocket,' he reminded.

'Slats Hooper?'

At the mention of the name Charlie swallowed heavily, and looked fearfully past me to be certain no-one could overhear.

'Cut out those names, will ya?' he squeaked.

'No more names,' I promised. 'But what about him, the last guy? A gambler carries a lot of green paper around all the time. He needs somebody to help him hang on to it.'

'Sure.' His voice dropped so low I had to bend forward to catch the hoarse words. 'He needs a heavy man, a muscle.

131

That's O.K. But he don't have to have somebody like — like he's got. It ain't necessary and it would cost too much. The asking price for a guy like that is three fifty, four hundred a week. Any ordinary muscle would get one fifty tops. So why spend that extra money? It don't make sense.'

I hadn't thought about it in those terms before, but Charlie was right. There was no doubt of it.

'That's neat thinking, Charlie. Why do you suppose the big fellow plays it that way?'

'Search me. Unless it was on account of Ears.'

I leaned against the wall next to him and digested that. Before Slats Hooper got the job of watching Ralfini's back, an ex-fighter named Ears Flanagan was doing it. Somebody got to Flanagan. They picked him up out in the desert one morning, and he was all through guarding anybody. He'd been pistol-whipped about the head and throat by experts, and the last I heard he would probably spend the rest of his life in a home. Slats was just out of jail, and he took over. That was about a month ago. I spoke to Charlie.

'You think that beating was meant as a warning to — to the gambling man?'

'I don't know. I don't know nothing,' he repeated doggedly. 'All I'm saying is what I hear. But the Ears didn't carry any iron. Ain't nobody gonna do to the new man what they done to him.'

'And you really don't know what it's all about? All right, all right,' as he opened his mouth to protest — 'what do you know about the gambler and a certain big shot bookie? What makes them so clubby?'

Charlie's face was ashen.

'That is one of the great mysteries of the day, Preston. And you may like to know you've already knocked ten years off my file with your lousy questions.'

I wasn't going to get any more. I patted him on the arm.

'Too bad you couldn't help, Charlie. Here's ten,' I pressed a ten-spot into his clutching hand. 'If you think of anything I might like to hear, there's another ten in my pocket. Call me any time.'

He nodded, glad to be seeing the last of me.

'You bet.'

I went out thoughtfully. The way things stood, I seemed to be picking up an awful lot of information that wasn't going to be any use. Not that I found that at all unusual. That's a large part of this job. You have to gather in all you can, and then try to decide which of the heap of facts is likely to be of any value, and which ones you can dump in the trash-can. What I needed was another talk with Julian Ventura. Stopping off at a liquor store, I picked up two bottles of scotch and headed for West 17th. Soon I was leaning on the buzzer of Apartment 310. There was no answer. I tried again, but without result. Checking that the corridor was empty I turned the handle of the door, and it opened. With two full bottles under my arm I couldn't free the .38 if it became necessary, but I took a chance on that. Stepping in, I looked around at the empty room, then closed the door. I stood the bottles on a table, and looked in the cabinet where the glasses had been on my last visit. If I was going to wait for Ventura and Arabella Bell, I might as well be comfortable. The cabinet was empty. They probably took the glasses to another room. I opened the bedroom door, and forgot about the glasses. Arabella was there. She was sitting in a chair, with her arms tied behind her. Her blouse had been ripped off in front, and the creamy flesh was marred by deep burns. She must have passed out a few times, because a half empty pail of water stood on the floor and water had been thrown into her face, as the sopping hair testified. Finally, Arabella had talked. Either that, or her tormentors had decided she couldn't or wouldn't. Because finally somebody had jerked back her head and driven an icepick deep into her throat. Her face was frozen in agony and terror. I took a few deep breaths, wiped sudden damp from my forehead. Then my stomach couldn't take it any more, and I spent the next five minutes in the john. After that I felt, not better, but more able to cope. This time I didn't bother to look for any glass. I broke the seal on the cap of the nearest bottle and tipped the stuff straight down. Having caught my breath, I gave myself a second shot. Then I went to the phone and called headquarters.

8

I was still sitting by the phone when they came. The whisky had dulled me a little, and for fifteen minutes I'd done nothing else but exclude from my mind the knowledge of what was in the room behind me.

Randall was first through the door, closely followed by his shadow, Detective First-Grade Schultz. They looked at me, then quickly around.

'Where?' demanded Randall.

I jerked a thumb over my shoulder and they went past into the bedroom. Randall came back alone.

'That her whisky?'

'No, it's mine.'

'H'm.'

He picked up the bottle, stuck it in his face and swallowed hugely. I watched curiously as he took the bottle away and wiped his lips.

'Nothing to stare at,' he barked.

'I don't recall I ever saw you drink on duty before,' I explained.

He nodded and put the bottle back on the table.

'That's right. And you're not seeing me now. I needed that to keep my stomach where it ought to be. Work to do. And I notice you've been nibbling some yourself.'

We were even.

'All right,' I said wearily. 'Neither of us is as tough as he used to be. Now what?'

'Now facts. Who's the dame?'

'Name of Arabella Bell.'

He looked up quickly from his notebook, saw it wasn't one of my joke days, and wrote it down. Schultz came and joined us then. Randall took one look at his face and passed over the scotch.

'Go ahead,' he instructed. 'Before the boss man gets here.'

Then he turned back to me.

'You know this Miss Bell?'

'Not really. I just saw her the one time.'

'We'll get to that. Tell me what happened here.'

'I came round to see a man who was

supposed to be at this address. Nobody answered the door, so I opened it.'

'You broke in? Why?'

'I didn't break in,' I contradicted. 'I merely opened the door.'

'That's breaking in,' he confirmed. 'But skip it for the present. You opened the door and?'

'There was nobody here. At least I didn't think so. Then I went in there and — and she was like that.'

'This was when?'

'Thirty minutes ago, no more.'

'Body discovered approx. five p.m. Tell about the man you came to see.'

I was sour on the whole thing. Maybe another day I'd have done better. Some day when I hadn't found what I found today.

'His name is Ventura, Julian Ventura.'

I gave a close description of the way he looked, and the clothes he was wearing when I last saw him. Randall looked at the pale Schultz.

'Anything?'

'No. Doesn't sound like one of our boys around town. Of course, names

139

don't mean a thing.'

Randall grunted and turned to me.

'What's with you and this Ventura?'

'That doesn't matter any more does it? What you have to do now is find him. Find out what he knows about that.'

'I saw her too,' growled the sergeant, 'and I don't need any fancy pants flatfoot telling me what I have to do. Your buddy Ventura, could he have done this?'

'He's not my buddy,' I denied automatically. 'And yes, he could have done it. I would say he's a tough monkey.'

'I know lots of tough monkeys. Not many of them could have done that in there. That takes a special kind of tough. Is your boy that special kind?'

'I don't know,' I said tiredly.

'How come you know the woman?' queried Schultz.

'I called here last night looking for Ventura. He wasn't here. The woman and I talked a few minutes. That's the only other time I've seen her.'

Randall jabbed a black pencil towards me.

'What does this Ventura do?'

140

'I don't know. I told you, I don't know anything about him except his name and description.'

'You touch anything here after you found her?'

Schultz again.

'No. You know me better than that.'

'Aha,' Randall cried triumphantly. 'Fake statement. You touched the bottle — '

'I brought the bottle with me,' I protested.

' — And you touched the telephone,' he continued. 'Now, are you sure there aren't one or two other little things you forgot?'

I told him about the time I spent in the bathroom.

'It's wonderful how memory comes back sometimes. Any other small items you overlooked? Did you wipe finger-prints off that ice-pick handle, little stuff like that?'

I was about to say something, when Rourke walked into the room.

'Where?' he rasped.

Schultz took him away. He was soon back, and I noticed a quick wistful glance at the bottle.

'What's he doing here?'

He spoke to Randall, and he meant me. Randall told him what he had so far.

'I want this Ventura, and quick. Get his name and description out on the radio. I want an identi-kit picture fast. Preston will help the artist. Schultz, get down to records and see what they can do. I'll have the prints sent down to you. Ah, about time.'

Randall and Schultz went out as the lab squad arrived. Men with small suitcases, and steel rules and cameras. Rourke waved them towards the bedroom.

'Not a very good week for you is it?'

'I've seen better.'

'I imagine. All right, I'd go along with the coincidence yesterday. Could be you just happened to be Johnny-on-the-spot when the little guy got bumped off. But this, today, I can't go for this. Two of 'em, two days, two ice-picks. You're in trouble, Preston.'

'Ridiculous,' I snapped. 'You know I could never do a thing like that in there. Never.'

'Sure I know it,' he nodded agreeably.

'I'm behind you one hundred per cent there. But I'm saying you know something. And I'm going to have that something, or you are going to spend some time as a guest of the city. Quite a lot of time, I imagine. So don't start trying to think up any wriggles Preston. I want what you have, I want it now. I want all of it, or I'm going to nail you to a tree. Just so we all know where we stand.'

He smiled pleasantly and sat down, waiting. I'd done business with this grizzled Irishman before, and I knew he meant it. Rourke is the kind of officer most cities would welcome with open arms. He was tough and intelligent, both at the same time. He was also incorruptible and he ran a clean squad. There had been periods when Monkton City had crooked administrations, but not even those had been able to shake Rourke from his determined path. Of course, in a fine city like ours, nothing is too good for an officer who has spent the greater part of thirty years tidying up its mess. So Rourke was head man of the Homicide Bureau, Captain of Detectives no less.

Naturally that is just a title, and doesn't carry the rank and pay. With all the money that has to be found for new jails, prisoners recreation and so forth, the city has to prune a little here and there. One of the here and theres was Rourke's pay. And so he stayed a lieutenant, holding down a captain's job.

This flashed quickly through my mind as he pulled from his pocket one of those objectionable little Spanish cigars of his. This he lit, as though he enjoyed it, and a swirl of stinging yellow smoke rose above his head.

'I was going to tell you anyway — ' I began.

'Fine. Never hurts to co-operate with the department. Let's hear it.'

'Yesterday, out at the track, I was around when this Rendell was dying.'

'How soon around?' he interjected.

'Same as I told Randall. I just made the finish. I wasn't even in the front row of people watching.'

'Go on.'

'I know better than to hang around while anything like that is going on. I got in the car and beat it. In the glove compartment I found this package.'

'Package. What kind ofpackage?'

'A yellow oilskin. Inside was a fifty dollar bill and a key. An Express Company key.'

Rourke's eyes squinted, but whether because the smoke was stinging or because he didn't believe me, I couldn't tell.

'I couldn't figure this at all. Then I chewed on it, and I decided I'd been hired. Somebody was paying fifty bucks for me to collect whatever it was in the deposit box.'

The squinted eyes were now slits.

'That's what you decided? You get many cuckoo clients like that?'

'Not too many. But I've had stranger assignments. It seemed to me the thing was to collect the stuff and keep it in my office till the owner claimed it.'

'Which you did,' his voice was suspicious. 'What was it?'

'I told you this was crazy. It was a package of papers, old papers. I took them back to the office. Five minutes after I sat down, this Ventura showed up.

He wanted the package, he said. He kind of emphasised the point by showing me a Colt .38.'

'He told you his name?'

'No, I'm coming to that. I was all set to hand the stuff over, because I never argue with a gun, particularly when the man has held one before. Right then I got a break. A friend of mine came in and dropped my visitor. I went through his pockets and found a driver's license made out to Julian Ventura.'

'Does this hero friend have a name?' asked Rourke politely.

'Sam Thompson.'

'I might just have guessed that. So Thompson rides in on his white horse. Then what?'

'I was interested in guys who get ready to shoot me for a parcel of junk. I asked Sam to find out about him. When Ventura came round I told him to beat it. He hadn't seen who hit him, so he wouldn't spot Sam for a tail. Sam came back later and told me Ventura had come here.'

'These papers, you have them with you?'

'No. It looked as though they might have quite some value, so I mailed them to General Delivery, and that's where they are now.'

He chewed savagely at the black weed shooting sparks around.

'You expect me to believe it?'

'I don't care whether you believe it. Those are all the facts,' I said irritably.

'Don't be snappish,' he warned. 'I could still have you held.'

I sighed.

'I don't care about that, either. I've had it. I wish I'd never seen the damn key or the damn papers. I wish I'd never seen Ventura, and I certainly wish I'd never seen that in there. None of this is any of my business, and I don't care what happens. All I want is out.'

Rourke looked at me with those penetrating eyes. Neither of us said any more. Then the lab boys began to emerge from the bedroom. The photographer was a new man, and he looked at me curiously.

'Was it him?' he asked.

I got up fast, hands clenching. Rourke

stepped in front of me in one smooth movement. Over his shoulder he barked.

'You got your pictures. Go and get busy on them. Preston, you sit down.'

I sat down.

'Something else about Ventura,' I muttered. 'The girl said he was a lush.'

'Find one that isn't,' rejoined the policeman. 'Still, it may help. Are you ready?'

'You mean I can go?'

'Ah, Preston, don't. I know I'm nothing but a dumb Irish flatfoot, but you shouldn't rub it in that way. When you go, I go. You know that.'

I looked at the grizzled face, and could read nothing.

'You're going to pinch me? What for?'

'I didn't say that,' he soothed. 'Not yet, anyway. No, we'll just take a little walk down to the post office and pick up those crummy old papers. Let's go.'

He had a few quiet words with the fingerprint man. I picked up the unopened bottle and Rourke tut-tutted.

'Sorry. You can claim it later. Nothing must be moved.'

Together we went downstairs and out

into the early evening sun.

'Now that we don't have any witnesses Mark, is that really the whole of it?' enquired Rourke.

'That's all there is. Except you'd better latch on to Ventura before I find him,' I said nastily.

'Enough of that talk,' he snapped. 'We don't even know he's our boy. And I don't need any imitation policeman playing God. I have enough trouble with this town as it is. You hear me?'

'I hear you.'

At the post office I claimed the letter and a large hand took it from me at once. Ripping open the envelope, Rourke shuffled quickly through the contents.

'And this is all? You didn't keep one or two choice pieces for yourself?'

'That's the way I found it. You through with me now?'

He tapped the envelope against his cheek and looked at me, making up his mind.

'I guess so. I've always been too soft-hearted. But even you have to have the benefit of the doubt sometimes.'

149

'What doubt?' I asked fiercely. 'Don't you talk that way to me, or I might just forget who you are.'

'You'd remember quick enough when you woke up in that little room with the bars,' he returned softly. 'Now get on your way, before I change my mind.'

I got, walking quickly back to the Chev and moving away before he really did have second thoughts. I went back to Parkside and called the office. Florence Digby said a man had been calling. He didn't give any name, but said to tell you he was the man I owed money. There was no return number, the man would call again. I told the Digby goodnight and put down the phone. I was wondering what Ventura was up to. My guess would have been that he'd clear out until the Arabella murder died down. Then I realised I wasn't thinking too well today. Rourke had been right. In my own mind I'd elected Ventura as Arabella's killer, and on the information I had, that wasn't very bright. Of course, he wasn't to know I knew of her death. That could be the answer. It could also be that he needed his roll back for getaway money. Just the same, I'd have to be a little more objective.

Stripping off my clothes I crawled under the shower and just stood there a few minutes, letting the warm rivulets wash away the taste and the feel of West 17th. After that I turned the control to full cold and jumped as the icy spikes drove against prickling skin. Shivering, I stepped out and began a rubdown job with a thick harsh towel. I felt better, much better, and I poured two fingers of scotch which made me better still. Then I stuck an Old Favorite in my face and that completed the cure. Towel wrapped around, I dug out fresh linen and a different suit. Ten minutes later I was all set for a night's work.

Francis O. Lishman was listed at a Pinetop address, which was the right end of town for a prominent man. Once clear of the city, it was a twenty minute ride along the beach highway. Up there on the cliffs, it was peaceful and picturesque. A place of quiet private roadways and houses well screened from the gaze of passers by. I found the white gate with the house name painted on it. Climbing out, I opened the gate and secured it to the little concrete post provided. Then I got back in the car, and drove up the approach road. The house was not as big as I'd imagined. I always expect people in the Lishman bracket to live in forty-roomed imitation castles with maybe a Viennese orchestra playing on the vast lawn. They seldom do, and the fact I can't shake the illusion is just another indication of my peasant roots. The Lishman house was more modest, maybe eight or nine rooms, and why not? How many rooms do one man and one daughter need? There was plenty of space for parking. I noted a small white two-seat continental job, one of these hundred plus machines that usually seem to be driven by people who are old enough to know better. Further along there was a Buick, and beyond that a big Ford station wagon. There was magnolia trailing all round the entrance to the porch and the scent hung heavily on the closed-in air as I rang the doorbell. A small oriental looking man in a white jacket opened the door and looked at me.

'Please?'

'Like to see Mr. Lishman if he's home. The name is Preston.'

'So sorry. Him come later. You come again maybe sometime soon.'

He was all set to shut the door when a woman's voice called:

'Who is it, Ling?'

'Gentleman for Mist Lishman. He come back again.'

'Wait a minute.'

She came to the door to see for herself. I was glad she did. Above average height, maybe five seven, she had the figure of an athlete, slim and well-proportioned. She walked with a free swinging stride and carried herself erect. Her face was cute rather than pretty, with a frame of short black hair. She was in her early twenties and she was a fine healthy looking girl.

'Hallo. I'm Betsy Lishman. Can I help?'

What was it Harve Mason said, a peacheroo? Well, he was right about Betsy.

'My name is Preston, Miss Lishman. Your father wanted to see me. I couldn't make it earlier today, so I came to the house. I hear I'm out of luck.'

She looked me over, deciding whether I'd be likely to steal the silver.

'What was it about?'

There was no suspicion in her voice, the question was routine.

'He wanted to see me about a job.'

'Oh.' She puckered up her mouth, and I would have liked to do something about that. But I knew the space was reserved for one Maurice Parker. 'Well, he'll be here any minute. Won't you come in and wait?'

Ling didn't seem too steamed up over the idea, but he stood back so I could get in.

'This way.'

Betsy strode away down the hall. Ling put a finger on my arm.

'Mister, why you got a gun, please?'

'I'm a deputy sheriff,' I replied seriously, and followed Betsy.

Ling was a sharp-eyed man to have around the house, I reflected. But people always seem to go for that badge routine. Not that it was untrue. Some years before I did a favor for the mayor of a small Mexican village and he made me a deputy sheriff on the spot, badge and all. As an official status it carried about as much weight as being axe-sharpener to some European king, but people like the sound of it.

Betsy Lishman was standing in the doorway of a large pine-walled room.

'In here Mr. Preston. Oh, Stella Delaney this is Mr. Preston. He's come to see my father.'

Stella Delaney looked up with amusement, and her eyes danced.

'Hallo, Mr. Preston.'

'Well, well, this must be my lucky day.'

'You two know each other?' queried Betsy.

'Oh yes,' replied Stella. 'Mr. Preston sells sea food.'

Betsy tried to look impressed. She wasn't very good at it.

'Oh really? That must be — er — very interesting.'

Stella wasn't going to let me down easily.

'Not for Mr. Preston. He isn't very good at it. You see he only tries to sell it to young females of edible age.'

'And,' I added solemnly, 'I always pick the ones who already have eating arrangements.'

'Oh,' said a relieved Betsy. 'In-jokes. That explains it. Will you have a drink Mr. Preston? There's a cocktail already mixed.'

'Thank you. I'd prefer scotch if you have it.'

'Of course.'

She splashed around, and I tried to avoid looking at Stella too much. It wasn't easy, because she kept on mocking me with her eyes. Betsy handed over a drink and I thanked her.

'Have you two had a row or something?' she demanded.

She had a forthright way of getting down to things which was disconcerting.

'Not at all,' replied Stella with a half-smile. 'Would you say we had had a row, Mr. Preston?'

'Why no, Miss Delaney,' I returned. 'I wouldn't say we had had very much of anything. Not yet, that is.'

Betsy snorted.

'I can't stand fencing. Would you people like me to go and hide somewhere so you can say whatever it is you want to say?'

I wasn't going to comment on that. I let Stella reply for the guests.

'No Betsy, of course not. There's nothing to make an issue about.'

I gulped some of my liquor and nodded. Then there was a noise outside.

'Father's home,' said Betsy with disappointment. 'And I'm sure I'd have gotten something out of you people in the next five minutes.'

The door opened, and I got my first look at Francis O. Lishman. He was not as tall as I, but broad like a barn and with a rugged face to match.

'You Preston? This way.'

I could see where Betsy Lishman got her plain speech. I swallowed my drink, smiled at the girls, and followed him out. He went to a room across the hall and flung open the door.

'Inside,' he barked.

I went in and the door shut with a bang.

'Mr. Lishman — ' I began.

That was all I said. A fist like a rock came from nowhere and smashed against the side of my face. I went down feeling nothing but surprise.

9

I opened one eye and looked at the ceiling. My jaw throbbed, and I put a hand to it tenderly. Then I sat up, still surprised. Lishman was sitting in a chair by the window, watching me. I climbed to my feet, realising I'd probably been out less than a minute. My head banged.

'Don't ever try that again,' I warned. 'Once is O.K. because I wasn't looking. From now on I'll be looking. And you're too old for this stuff Lishman. I don't want to have to spread you all over the wall.'

He sneered.

'Like this time? And how far would you get without this?'

From his knee he raised a .38 caliber Police Special which ought to have been under my arm.

'I don't get it,' I confessed. 'What's it all about?'

'Don't give me that,' he snapped. 'I

159

know why you're here. And you brought this along in case I got argumentative. Lucky for me Ling spotted it.'

My head was clear now. The jaw might bruise, but otherwise I'd survive. I turned a chair so it faced him, and sat down.

'All right,' I said. 'You know why I'm here. Tell me about it.'

He squinted suspiciously.

'You're here for money, and we both know it. I'll tell you this. You keep the price reasonable, and I'll pay it. But if you get too ambitious, I won't pay. And there won't be a thing you can do about it, because there are some people I know who'll know exactly what to do with you.'

'You must know some funny people for a business man,' I observed.

'I do. You think I'm bluffing you, try me. I've been pushed as far as a man can go, Preston. Now I'm fighting. And in a game like this, I'll fight as dirty as I have to.'

I nodded as though that made sense. I wished it did. I didn't have the remotest idea what we were talking about.

'All right Preston, that's the picture. Talk money.'

'Glad to. It's one of my favorite subjects,' I told him. 'The only problem is, I don't know what you're talking about.'

'Huh?'

He put his head to one side to get a better look at me.

'I'll say it again. I don't know what you're talking about.'

'I don't believe you,' he rapped.

I shrugged.

'You can do as you damn please. The fact remains.'

With the .38 in his hand, he scraped thoughtfully at an ear.

'All right,' he said slowly. 'Tell me what you're doing here.'

'If you'd asked me that in the first place we could have cut out all this comedy,' I pointed out.

'I like it better the way it is,' he replied. 'Especially I prefer to be the one with the gun. Let's hear your fairy story.'

I lit a cigaret and blew smoke upwards.

'I want to ask you a question. You offered me a job today. Why?'

The question took him by surprise.

Again he rasped the gun against his ear. It was obvious from the look on his face that he couldn't decide what answer to make. Finally he hedged.

'What job?'

'Come on, Lishman. I know you're a big busy man and all that, but you don't hire so many private investigators that you can't remember all the way back to this morning.'

'I don't know anything about it. Maybe one of the office force — '

'No,' I cut in. 'You did it personally. I checked. Now I have two questions. Why are you lying about it now?'

'You watch your tongue,' he warned.

'Oh pooh,' I chided. 'Don't try talking tough at me. That's my daily hazard, only it's usually done by experts. Try answering the questions instead.'

'I — may have called myself,' he said hesitantly.

'I know that. I'm asking you why.'

He laughed, but it wasn't a confident sound.

'Well, I should have thought that was obvious enough. A job needed doing. I asked around, and your name came up. A simple matter of business.'

'There's nothing simple about any business that pays the kind of money you were offering me,' I pointed out.

'That? Well, that's soon told. The project is costing a fortune. It's well worth that money to get the delays stopped. The job needs doing fast and properly.'

The ache in my jaw was beginning to ease.

'O.K.' I nodded, apparently satisfied. 'Delaney told you I wasn't available?'

'He did.'

'Mind telling me who got the job?'

He wasn't ready for it.

'Why nobody, I haven't had time to — er — '

He floundered and I showed him a wide smile.

'So you haven't had time. The big important investigation is only big and important when you want me for it. That how it reads? When I can't do it, you find you haven't the time to get another boy? And then, when I come to talk to you,

you find time to slug me and steal my gun? Is that what you always do to people who won't work for you?'

Lishman got up and put the gun in his pocket. Progress.

'Look, Preston, I have to think. I'm going to have a drink. Do you want one?'

'Will it be poisoned?' I demanded.

He flushed and opened a door in a bookcase. Then he poured himself something and drained the glass at one gulp. With his back to me, he rested his hands on a shelf and dropped his head towards his chest. Then he took a deep breath and came back to his chair.

'Is this on the level?' he asked quietly. 'That's really why you came here today?'

'That's the reason,' I confirmed. 'Of course, I now have a bagful of other questions.'

Till now, he'd been all determination. He knew what he was doing, what he was up against, and he'd been equal to it. I kicked away his reasons, and that left him dangling. With confidence oozed out, he now had a hunted look, but it was too early in the game for me to feel anything about that. I've seen the same look on the faces of three-time losers with their backs against a fence in an alley.

'Look Preston, I may have made a mistake. That may sound a feeble excuse for acting the way I did, but believe me I've been having a hell of a time just lately. All I can do is apologise, and I'll be glad to pay for your inconvenience — '

I laughed at the sheer effrontery of the man.

'Great. Just great. That's all you need to do, is it, just say you're sorry and sprinkle a few dollars around? Well, it won't do this time.'

At once he was watchful again.

'Well, what do you want?'

'Answers,' I replied briefly.

'I doubt whether I can help you very much.'

'Oh, I don't have any doubts about that at all. All my doubts are as to whether you will help, not whether you can. Now, about that job.'

'I told you. We needed a good man — '

'Correction,' I butted in. 'You needed one particular good man. Me. With me

165

not available, suddenly all the urgency disappears.'

He didn't reply, but sat staring at a fixed point over my left shoulder.

'All right,' I decided. 'Have it your way. I came out here hoping to get some information that would help me. You're not handing out any help these days, O.K. Just don't come crying to me when this thing blows up.'

'What thing? I don't follow you.'

'I think you do. I think you could put me a jump or two ahead in the game, but you don't choose to. There's been murder done, Lishman.'

His eyebrows jumped. He was either a first-class liar, or I was bringing him news.

'Murder,' I repeated. 'And not just one murder. Anybody might overlook just one little old murder. We already have two behind us, and more to come for all I know.'

He looked away from me again.

'I don't believe you.'

'Read the papers. You believe me all right. What you mean is, you don't want it

166

to be true. But that won't change anything. Two people are dead, and they'll stay that way. You know Julian Ventura's back in town?'

I got the eyebrows again.

'Who? None of this makes any sense to me.'

Whether he was lying or not, there was no way of telling. He certainly looked puzzled enough.

'Julian Ventura,' I repeated. 'Mention him to the King and Lucky Hertz. They'll know him.'

There was no evasion this time. Instead he looked guilty as hell.

'What makes you think I know those people?' he mumbled.

'Well, that's about all I can take of this.'

I got up and went across with my hand out.

'I'll take the gun now.'

He hesitated, then slid a hand into his pocket and came up with my old friend. I took it and put it where it belonged.

'Think about our little chat,' I suggested. 'We could talk some more if you wanted. But only if you've got something to say besides oh and ah.'

Turning, I went to the door.

'Preston.'

He called in a low voice, the voice of a man who needed help. I didn't know what the help might be for.

'Yeah?'

Lishman shook his head.

'Nothing.'

I shrugged and went out. Somehow, I had a feeling I'd played it wrong. Somewhere along the line I missed a cue, and after that there was no replay for Lishman and Preston. Slightly annoyed with myself, I went out of the house.

Stella Delaney was sitting in the diminutive white sport car. She waved as though I might miss her.

'Hallo again.'

I walked over and stood looking down at her. She looked good enough to eat, blonde curls stirring in the light breeze, and one of those lopsided smiles on the beautiful lips.

'We seem to have spent most of the day together, Miss Delaney,' I told her.

'Amazing how our paths seem to cross,' she agreed.

'Where would your path be around nine tonight?' I queried.

She shook her head and the late sun glinted on white teeth.

'Sorry, I really do have a dinner date.'

'Too bad. Well, some other time.'

I began to walk away, but she leaned over the side of the car, and put a hand on my arm.

'But it isn't till eight-thirty,' she told me. 'You could offer to buy a lady a drink.'

I grinned, and not entirely with self-satisfaction.

'Miss Delaney you have a deal. You know the Yachtsman?'

'Yup. See you there in ten minutes.'

The car leaped away from underneath me, and she disappeared down the drive. I climbed aboard the Chev and pointed it west. I didn't see her once along the road, although I gunned the motor hard most of the way. When I reached the Yachtsman, there was her car, neatly parked close by the front entrance.

I found her at a window table, nursing a tall frosted glass and staring out at the smooth ocean.

'Is this seat taken?' I asked.

She turned and looked up at me thoughtfully.

'I thought you'd changed your mind.'

I chuckled and sat down.

'You certainly toss that heap around don't you? Are you any good, or just fast?'

'I'm good,' she returned casually. 'Barney Westmoor wanted me for his team two years ago, but I couldn't do it for family reasons.'

'Tough luck. Barney's a wonderful champion, you'd have learned a lot. Now you just drive for laughs, huh?'

'You make it sound unattractive,' she accused.

Unattractive was a word that hadn't any business in the same room with Stella Delaney.

'Lady, I don't want to say anything at all that might lead to a misunderstanding with you. Let's change the subject. Why do you hold down a job at Delaney, This and That?'

The waiter interrupted, and went away for fresh drinks. Stella looked at me with amusement.

'Why shouldn't I? I'm just a working gal.'

'From choice,' I pointed out. 'I don't imagine the family is close to destitution. What I meant was, why work in the family business? You could do almost anything you want.'

'True.' She looked at the glass topped table, and traced a pattern with her forefinger, the way she had in the restaurant earlier. 'The trouble is, there isn't very much of anything I want to do. So I stay in the office. It fills up the days.'

There was something else there, something she didn't want to talk about. And it wasn't any of my business. I decided to concentrate on things that might become my business.

'So much for the days, all nicely filled out. How about the evenings, any gaps there?'

She smiled in that lazy way of hers, and I was making progress. The waiter chose that moment to arrive with our order.

'You looked as though you could have strangled that poor man,' she mocked, when he'd gone.

'Why shouldn't I?' I asked. 'Just as you were about to make an important announcement. What was it, by the way?'

'Something about the evenings,' she pretended to recall. 'I know, you asked how I filled those in.'

'And the answer was what?'

'I go out and around. I meet people. What did you want me to say, I stay in an ivory box at home?'

'I'm not much for ivory boxes myself,' I admitted. 'And in your case I wouldn't have believed it anyway.'

'You ask a lot of questions,' she accused.

'Second nature. It's a large part of my job.'

'Yes, I was going to ask about that.'

People always do. But I let her ask away, and the waiter seemed to come and go a few times, and we talked about this and that. We were old friends when she finally looked at her watch.

'I should have left twenty minutes ago,'

she said, but it didn't appear to worry her much. 'Now I really must go.'

I said must she really, and she said yes she really must, and so I went out with her and watched a small white car become a shrinking blob on the highway. I hoped the outcome of what I was going to do wouldn't make her decide I was bad news.

It was almost nine in the evening and I had to go see one or two people before the hard daily round was over. Fortunately I knew where to find King Ralfini and his shadow, Slats Hooper. The King always took his food between nine and ten o'clock at a place rejoicing in the name of the Oyster's Cloister. I left the heap outside and winked at the huge doorman.

'Hi, Biff.'

'Well, Mr. Preston. Been a long time.'

His ugly face creased in a smile. Biff has two smiles. One is for the dollar customers, and it means I hope you have a good time in there and I'll be around to pick up the loose change as you leave. The other smile means I'm glad to see you, and this was the one Biff handed me. Inside the place I poked my head round the door of the manager's office. Reuben Krantz looked up with his customary glare, switched off thirty per cent of it when he saw who it was.

'It ain't bad enough I'm balancing the books,' he groaned. 'For extra duty they send you.'

I went in and closed the door.

'It's nice to see you again too after all these months,' I told him.

'My pleasure. How's the stomach?'

He waved me to silence with a horrified hand.

'Don't mention that word around here. Nobody would believe the way I suffer. Why, just two nights back I had to go home at three.'

I nodded in sympathy. Krantz's stomach is generally accepted as being one of the things that should never have happened to the twentieth century.

'I heard of a new thing the other day,' I said, trying to remember.

'You take it in milk.'

There was a silver pencil poised in his

hand before I finished speaking.

'Well, go on, let's have the details.'

I told him the name of the stuff as near as I could recall. He scribbled anxiously, as I'd known he would. The druggists in Monkton City are among the most prosperous people in the community. Ninety per cent of their prosperity is due to Krantz.

'If it works out I'll send you a crate of champagne,' he promised.

'Deal.'

'So what can I do for you, Preston?'

'Just social,' I replied carefully. 'Came to chat with a couple of your customers. Thought you'd like to know I was around.'

'Thoughtful. You was always thoughtful. These customers, you wouldn't tell me their names?'

I told him, and his face grew even more strained.

'I wouldn't be about to have a mess of trouble out there, would I? Thing like that soon gets around. People stop coming, you know how it is.'

'I know how it is. And I don't expect any trouble.'

He took a small tin from a drawer, put three large tablets in his mouth and gulped noisily at water he poured from a silver pitcher. Then he screwed up his face and pressed a hand to his middle.

'There's hell going on down there tonight,' he advised me sadly. 'And don't tell me you don't expect trouble. You don't need to. Trouble follows you around like you was some kind of magnet. If I had any sense I'd bar you from the joint.'

A man with stomach trouble is apt to take a jaundiced view of the world.

'I knew you'd understand,' I said, standing in the doorway. 'Let me know how the cure comes out.'

I bought a drink standing up at the bar and had a look at the diners. The boys I was looking for had a side-table. Ralfini's back was to me, but Slats Hooper sat where he could watch the door. That would have been what I'd expect. They weren't quite finished eating, and I didn't want any interruptions from waiters while we were talking. Slats was not over big, and looked even smaller sitting down. He had a thin, starved-looking face and the thick spectacles did nothing to enhance his attractions. As he ate, his head roved continually from side to side. He made me think of some bird of prey, feeding on carrion and watching for enemies. He seemed to peck at his food, rather than eat it. His boss was an entirely different proposition. The great back was hunched forward over the table, and he shovelled in the goodies with a steady rhythmic motion, punctuated regularly by large draughts from the huge chianti bottle in front of him. They made an interesting contrast sitting there.

I nibbled slowly at my drink, paying little attention to what was going on around. There was one trio of people that would have been fun to follow through the evening, two men and a woman. One was a noisy character named Tom, the woman was his wife, and the other man was a friend of the family. The woman sat between them, and Tom was giving his opinions on most subjects plenty of air. The part I would have liked to hear was Tom's opinion on the fact that his wife was playing considerable footsie with the friend of the family beneath the table.

After a while the boys I'd come to see had finished eating. As the waiters cleared away I walked across and sat down. Slats looked at me as though I'd crawled from under a stone.

'The seat's taken, slob. Beat it.'

Ralfini beamed, good humour and gold teeth breaking out all over his face.

'Say, I know you. It's Preston ain't it? You're the eye.'

'That's who I am,' I confirmed.

Slats was not impressed.

'The seat is still taken. Blow before I bend it over your head.'

I ignored him and talked to the fat man.

'You ought to get another dog, King. This one smells.'

Slats breathed heavily, but otherwise showed no emotion. Ralfini chuckled as though enjoying himself.

'You ought to watch your manners my friend. This dog, he don't have no bark at all. He's all bite.'

I nodded and tapped an Old Favorite.

'That's what I came to see you about.

You've been lousing up my apartment. It may not have been this particular mongrel, but it was some of your pack. Why?'

Ralfini took a huge silver case from an inside pocket and drew out a big cigar. We all had the pleasure of watching while he stripped the foil, and went to work with a silver cutter. Finally he was satisfied, set light to the huge weed and grunted. Looking at me from behind lowered fleshy eyelids, he said:

'I'm a very busy man, Preston. Ask anybody, they'll tell you the same. The King, they'll tell you, he's a busy man. But, a funny thing, I always got time to talk business. Did you come here to talk business, or just to talk?'

'Business is better,' I replied. 'What kind of business did you have in mind?'

'What other kind is there?' he shrugged. 'Money business.'

'O.K. That suits me fine. I'll take two hundred bucks.'

Pausing in mid-puff, the King opened his eyes wider. Even Slats seemed taken aback.

'Two *hundred?*' queried the big man.

'A clown,' grumbled Slats. 'That must be for the popcorn concession.'

Ralfini's face darkened swiftly and there was no good humor when he spoke to his henchman.

'You shut up and stay shut. This guy knows his business. If he says two hundred, that's what he means. You got a deal, Preston.'

I held out my hand.

'Good. Let's have the money.'

He wagged a forefinger like a sausage.

'Not so fast,' he demurred. 'How about the merchandise?'

'Huh?'

I looked at him blankly.

'The merchandise,' he growled. 'You don't imagine I'm going to give you any money without the stuff?'

'King,' and I sounded bewildered, 'I'm not tuned to your beam. I don't know about any merchandise.'

'Ah.'

He drummed on the table and looked enquiringly at Slats.

'Tell me something, peeper. Why would

I want to give you two hundred bucks?'

'I thought we both knew that,' I said openly. 'It's to compensate for the damage your pigs did when they turned my place over.'

Ralfini drew in breath in a deep hiss.

'Too bad you weren't in it,' muttered Slats. 'I told you this guy was a clown.'

'And I told you to clam up,' the King reminded him. Then he turned back to me. He was still grinning, but all the laughter was on his mouth, none in his eyes. 'People told me you were a smart feller, Preston. People can be wrong. Beat it. I got nothing to say to you.'

'Good. Then you'll be free to listen while I do the talking. I want you to know I'm in this. And my share is the big share, because I have what it takes to make me top man.'

'So you do have it?' he butted in.

'Maybe. Oh, and keep your pigs out of my apartment. There's nothing there, and I don't like having to fumigate the place all the time.'

Slats leaned forward, very white around the eyes.

'Don't walk down no alleys,' he warned. 'I'll be waiting for you.'

'What's your proposition, Preston?' demanded his boss.

'I've been thinking it over. There's plenty for everybody. What are we quarrelling about? I'll just take my slice, a nice big slice, but I won't crowd everybody else out. What do you say?'

The ash was close to two inches long on the big cigar. Any emotions Ralfini may or not feel did not affect his hands.

'I got a better idea,' he said quietly. 'I give you to some friends of mine, and that gets you out of everybody's hair.'

'Uh uh,' I negatived. 'I thought of that. It'll just step up the heat. I'd be the third corpse. That won't encourage the police to drop their investigations now will it?'

'Third? What you talking about?'

'I'm talking about Race Rendell and the dame. That's two already. That would make me about third, wouldn't you say?'

Ralfini poured himself some more wine and gulped noisily.

'I heard about Race, that was over at

Palmtrees. But who is this dame you're talking about?'

'Her name is or was Arabella Bell. Sounds ridiculous doesn't it. It'll look bad on a tombstone.'

'Never heard of her,' asserted the King with finality.

'Maybe not. But she was Julian Ventura's girl friend. Cops are looking for him now.'

Gently, almost tenderly, the banana bunch hands separated the long ash from the glowing cigar end.

'That name was what?'

'Ventura. You've heard it before.'

Slats began to speak but a look from Ralfini drove him back into sullen silence.

'This Ventura, he bumped off the dame, huh? He prob'ly killed poor little Race, too. Where's my problem?'

'Here it is,' I informed him. 'Ventura has a watertight alibi for the girl's murder. The two killings go together, so he couldn't have fixed Race either.'

'That's on the level? About the alibi?'

'Yeah.'

'Then why are the cops looking for

him?' he asked quickly, and with obvious triumph.

'Because,' I explained carefully, 'they don't know about the alibi yet. When they do, they'll have to start over. That's where my idea comes in.'

Slats could hold himself in no longer.

'Look, why are you chinning with this creep? Let's get him outside and have a long talk with him.'

'And miss my beautiful idea?' I chided.

'What's with this idea of yours?' queried Ralfini.

Triumph on my face I leaned forward and spoke low.

'I have the package. That puts me in.'

'Or on a slab,' corrected the King.

'Maybe. But I still have it. The only dark cloud in the blue sky above is these killings. You know how the police are, especially Rourke. They keep poking around, asking questions, making things tough for business.'

'That Rourke,' growled the fat man. 'Some day I fix him good.'

'That won't change anything,' I pointed out. 'The investigation will still go on.

There's only one way to stop it for always.'

'I'm listening.'

'We give 'em Slats,' I concluded.

Hooper started in his chair.

'Hey — ' he began.

'Shut up.'

King Ralfini sat back and looked at Slats' face. It was worth a look at that moment. Then he looked at me, and he started to laugh. Deep, internal convulsions that brought tears running down the pudgy cheeks. The huge mass of his body shook and heaved while he enjoyed himself. Twice he began to say something, and twice a fresh paroxysm seized him and choked off his breath.

'Preston, I wanta thank you. That's the best laugh I've had in weeks. A beauty. You got any more like that?'

'Sure,' I beamed. 'Try this one. If you don't want to help with this, if you want to be against me, I'll tip off the police alone. And I'll tell them you're mixed up in it too. After that, I'll just take over the whole gravy train myself.'

'King, are you gonna sit there listening

185

to this loud-mouth?'

Without looking at Hooper, Ralfini spoke between lips almost closed.

'That's the last time I'm gonna be nice telling you to button your lip, Slats. The last time. Preston, you interest me. Nobody could be quite as crazy as you seem to be. Nobody who's still healthy.'

'What's crazy?' I demanded seriously. 'The police call off the dogs, we all get our feet in the cream. Sounds like a fine way out to me.'

'No,' he returned. 'You're forgetting Slats. What about Slats' feet? Won't be no cream on them, not the way you tell it. All he'd get would be a few pellets of cyanide, and who needs it? Anyhow, it's crazy. Slats don't know nothing about those things. He's got alibis too. Cops ain't that dumb.'

I tapped confidentially at the side of my nose, to show that more wisdom was on the way.

'You didn't let me finish,' I remonstrated. 'I don't mean we should turn Slats in. If we did, he'd only get off, and we'd be no further forward. What I meant was, let's feed the cops information that Slats is their boy. Meantime, you stake him and he blows town. Wherever he goes, you send his cut every month. Police'll keep looking for him, won't bother anybody else. It's great all round.'

This time the King was slower to come back. He had a thoughtful look at Hooper before he spoke.

'But suppose they catch up with him? What then?'

'Why, then he gets off just the same, and there's no harm done. We wouldn't be any worse off than we are right now, and at least we would have tried. After all, it wouldn't cost a nickel to try.'

'Yeah, but there's a flea in the bed. You.'

'Me?'

'Sure. Every way you tell the story, you're still in there with your hands out. Keep cutting yourself in. I don't think there's room.'

I laughed, to show he wasn't the only one who liked a joke.

'Sure I'm in. You forget, I'm the one with the stuff. I have to be in.'

'In the morgue, maybe?'

'I thought we finished with that kind of talk twenty minutes ago. The morgue is too busy now. It doesn't need more business and neither do you. Well, that's where I stand. Think over my idea about Slats. I'll be here same time tomorrow night to find out where you stand.'

I got up and pushed the chair back into place. Slats' eyes followed everything I did, every move I made, like a cobra watching a rabbit.

'You're leaving? You don't spend a lot of time talking things over, do you?' queried Ralfini softly.

'Not much. There's nothing to talk about, not really. I have the stuff, I call the play. It's as easy as that. Better get Slats a travel guide.'

'I have to talk to other people,' demurred the King.

'So talk to 'em. Before tomorrow night. Here.'

I wended my way between the tables. Out in the bar the jockey waved me over.

'You missed all the fun,' he told me. 'While you were talking to your friends we had a wrestling match.'

'Oh.'

'Sure,' he said enthusiastically. 'You probably didn't notice, but there was a guy and his wife sitting with this other guy. Seems the other guy and the wife were playing carpetbaggers under the table. The husband character finally got wise to this and started batting the both of 'em around. It wasn't long, but it was a good bout.'

I tutted.

'I always miss all the fun,' I complained.

10

There's one golden rule in my business. When you don't know what you're talking about, keep talking. In this caper for instance, I didn't know Tuesday from Christmas. Every time I thought a little daylight was beginning to show through, somebody plugged up the hole. So I kept on talking, making a lot of noise round and about. Letting everybody not forget that there was one M. Preston to be counted in any reckoning they might be doing. So far I'd made contact with everyone whose name had been mentioned, and providing there wasn't someone else, someone who hadn't figured yet, I ought to have worried at least one of them. True enough I hadn't paid any social call on Lucky Hertz, but I wasn't concerned about that. Ralfini or Hooper or Lishman would soon remedy the omission. Maybe all three of them, for all I knew.

The only difficulty with the keep

talking method when there's murder around, is you might make the killer jumpy. He might figure you as a guy who knows more than is healthy. Once a killer starts thinking that way, he only has one obvious solution. That is, to put the know-it-all character in the morgue. My first concern at that moment had to be to avoid this. I went to a crummy rooming house down on Fourteenth Street and walked in. There was a misshapen old man reading a newspaper that looked like it might have been rescued from a trash can. The old guy was in need of a bath and a shave. Make that several baths. He looked me over knowingly, noticing the clothes.

'Want two rooms,' I told him tersely. 'One for me, one for my friend.'

He peered over my shoulder.

'No ladies,' he muttered wheezily. 'House rule.'

It didn't take a lot of brains to gather from his tone that two dollars would break the house rule.

'I didn't mention a lady,' I snapped. 'My friend will get here later. Two rooms, next to each other.'

'This ain't the Ritz,' he grumbled. 'You'll have to take what's left.'

I leaned over very close to him and my nostrils writhed in protest.

'It's the Ritz if I say so dad,' I said unpleasantly. 'Now you just get rustling on those rooms before you accidentally get smeared all over the wall.'

His eyes bulged with fear and he swallowed twice in rapid succession.

'Sure, right away mister. Whatever you say.'

'That's right, dad, whatever I say. And remember when Julie Ventura wants something he gets it. You hear what I'm telling you?'

He was jangling keys nervously and getting them all jumbled up.

'Sure, you bet Mr. Ventura. I gotcha. C'm on and I'll take you up.'

The stale air smelled like spring as his body moved three feet away.

He led me up the worn stairs to the second floor.

'Just see how you like these two Mr. Ventura.'

He opened doors and I looked quickly at each room in turn. Then I turned on him with angry eyes.

'What's this, a pig-sty? You better find something better, and quick.'

As I moved towards him, he flattened himself against the wall, shivering with fright.

'These are the best in the house Mr. Ventura. Honest to God, the very best in the place.'

I paused, and looked disgusted.

'What a fleabag,' I said contemptuously. 'If I thought you was kidding me — '

'Honest Mr. Ventura, I wouldn't do a thing like that.'

'All right, inside and shut the door.'

He looked then as though he might pass out.

'I'm not gonna hurt you,' I told him. 'Get in there.'

Nodding furiously, he dived into the nearest room. I followed, and then he closed the door. Reluctantly. He cheered up a lot when I took money from my pocket.

'Here,' I handed him five dollars. 'Ventura always pays. I'm gonna be stopping over a while, and I like things quiet. There may be some guys around asking if you've seen me. You haven't. Kabish?'

Again he gave me that rapid nodding. He understood the whole thing now. I was on the run, either from some mob or the law. And the way I'd treated him, it would be a real pleasure to turn me over to either one.

'Now get back down there, and remember. You never heard of anybody named Ventura, and there are no strangers here. You behave yourself, there's another five in it for you tomorrow night. Get out.'

He got. His head was still nodding when the door closed. Almost at once it opened again.

'What about your friend, Mr. Ventura? If I ain't supposed to tell anybody — '

'He won't ask for me,' I informed him. 'He'll just say where's the room. You tell him.'

He hesitated, as though there was something else.

'If there's any little thing I can do for you? Some booze, or maybe you'd like a little company?'

'Nothing. Shut the door when you go. And don't come back.'

After he'd gone I sat on the bed, and it groaned dismally. I hadn't picked much of a place to stay. I also wasn't very clear whether I had such a wonderful idea using Ventura's name. Maybe there wouldn't be anybody looking for him at all. Except the police of course, and I didn't especially want to attract their attention. But it was just one more small thing to do, so I did it. One thing was certain, I wasn't going to wait around all night on the remote chance of action. I'd have to be out and around, showing my face. I'd picked the room with the fire escape. Now I eased up the window and stepped out onto rusting metal. Climbing carefully down, I made it to the street. Then I walked around the corner and got into the Chev. It took over half an hour to find Sam Thompson. He was perched over a moody glass of beer in a dingy bar down near the docks.

'Preston,' he greeted almost enthusiastically. 'Now I can afford a real drink. If you have any money, that is.'

I called the bartender across.

'What's the best scotch in the place?' I demanded.

The bartender looked crafty.

'Well now, that's a tough one. I got most of 'em here. Come to think, there may be just one bottle left of Uncles Bagpipes.'

'I'll take it.'

Thompson watched with mixed pleasure and suspicion as I paid for the bottle and tucked it under one arm.

'Couldn't we drink it here and be sociable?' he entreated.

'Sorry Sam. Duty calls. But you can nibble on this beauty while you're doing it.'

'With you there's always a tag,' he grumbled.

We went out to the car and got in. I had a pull at the Bagpipes and found it mellow and smooth. Then Thompson tipped the bottle up and splashed a good measure inside him.

'You buy good booze,' he sighed. 'I'll have to give you that. What's all this unpleasantness about work?'

I told him what had been going on since I saw him. He asked a few questions, grunted every now and then.

'I don't get the Fourteenth Street routine,' he announced at the end.

'What's it all about? Pushing this old bozo around, and making noises like Ventura?'

'Probably a waste of time,' I admitted. 'All I know is, Ventura is loose somewhere. I'm hoping certain people have put out the word on him. If they have they won't have overlooked Fourteenth Street. The only place he can go with no bags and almost no money would have to be a firetrap like that.'

Thompson nodded.

'O.K. A long shot, but you may make a score. The only part that don't make any sense at all, is why you go to all that trouble and then duck out the back way. Seems to me if you're going to make any profit out of a long shot like that, you'd have to stick around the pad and see who came calling. Oh no.'

Now he could make out the pattern. I patted him on the shoulder.

'That's it, Sam. That's why we're having this little chat. I knew you'd understand. I can't just stay there on a slim chance like that. I have to be out and around.'

He took another pull at the bottle and made a face.

'Natch,' he grumbled. 'You're out and around and I'm stuck in some smelly hole waiting for somebody to come and put a slug in me.'

'That's why I paid for the drinks,' I said smugly. 'They say alcohol deadens the pain.'

'This will cost you, if I live to collect,' he told me resignedly.

'Don't be such a worrier. Probably you'll just get a good night's rest.'

'Well O.K. Let's get it done.'

I took him to the rear of the rooming house.

'There's a door around the other side,' he mentioned.

'You were never one to look for the

easy way Sam,' I said solemnly. 'Here we have a nice fire escape. You can arrive incognito.'

He clambered out of the car protesting sadly about the kind of world we had where people like Thompson did all the hard work, while certain other people led a fat easy life. He was still muttering as he mounted upwards and merged in the surrounding gloom.

I headed for the nearest phone booth and called headquarters. After some arguments and clicking noises in my ear I got through to Randall.

'That you, Preston? Listen, you're supposed to call in and make a statement.'

'Going to, going to,' I assured him. 'I've just called you to find out how you're making out with Ventura.'

'What was that name again?' he stalled.

'Come on Randall, be nice. You wouldn't even have known there was such a guy if I hadn't tipped you off. With all this hot information I give you, the least you can do is tell me what's cooking.'

He paused, and I could visualise him

staring at the ceiling, turning it over in his mind.

'Ventura, you say?'

'That's what I say.'

'Sure, we have a customer by that name,' he said guardedly.

'A customer? You mean you've got him?'

He sighed. At least, it started out as a sigh at his end. Over the phone it sounded like a big wave crashing against rocks.

'That's what it usually means. You'll have to pardon the police vernacular.'

'Has he been charged with the girl's murder? Has he said anything?'

The rocks took another beating.

'Why is it the public can never get it in their heads that a murder charge is serious business,' he said regretfully. 'You can't just yank anybody in off the street and book him for murder. It isn't polite — '

'But you are holding him?' I pressed. 'Listen, don't forget it was me saw that girl first. My stomach's still jumping.'

'All right,' he relented. 'Because it's

200

been a long day and I'm not so sharp as I ought to be. Your boy is down at the Fourth Precinct house. We're holding him on an attempted robbery charge.'

I thought I must have a bad connection.

'A what charge?'

'Attempted robbery. He tried to knock off a late drug store about an hour ago. Local boys got him. Rourke will be going down there to ask one or two little questions about the other matter.'

I thanked him and hung up. Then I dug around in my pockets for more change. The next man I called was lawyer Irving Hughes.

'Who? Preston? Oh yes, I remember you. It's very late Mr. Preston.'

'So it is, Mr. Hughes, but this is urgent. There's a man named Ventura, Julian Ventura, down at the Fourth Precinct. The police have him on an attempted robbery charge. Want you to go and get him out.'

His reply was barely civil.

'Really? I have an office, Mr. Preston. Also a secretary and an appointment

201

book. I believe the number is listed.'

'Wait, please. Tomorrow will not be soon enough. We have to get Ventura out tonight.'

'Mr. Preston, fortunately I know you and I know your reputation. But for that I would have slammed the phone down before this. I don't see what can be so urgent that it can't wait till morning. If you haven't any further explanation, I'm afraid I can't help you.'

He meant it, and I knew I'd have to take a chance.

'This will have to be in strict confidence, Mr. Hughes. I am acting on instructions from Clifford Delaney personally. You don't want me to fill that out?'

He didn't reply immediately. What he was doing, I knew, was trying to puzzle out how Clifford Delaney, of Delaney, etc., etc., could possibly have any interest in some bum on an attempted robbery squeal.

'Really?' he said at last. 'Mr. Clifford Delaney?'

'Really,' I confirmed. 'I couldn't understand why he had to have any lawyer.

After all, his firm is one of the oldest in this part of the state. I would have thought all he would do would be to pick up the telephone. But he didn't want to do that.'

Hughes chuckled knowingly.

'Ah no, naturally not. I'm afraid you are not too well informed about the legal profession Mr. Preston. We have our specialists, just as in medicine. This kind of work is not at all in Mr. Delaney's normal field. Not that he could not do it, I am not suggesting that for a moment. Mr. Delaney is a most-ah-proficient and respected figure. But this is not his field. No sir.'

'That's what he said, something like that. Said it wouldn't be right for him to encroach on the field. It would have to be done by someone well known in this line. He mentioned you.'

I wished I could see Hughes' face. He was probably looking at himself in the mirror.

'Mentioned me? Really? Mentioned my name?'

He'd heard me right the first time, but

he wanted to hear it again. And a few embellishments would not be unacceptable.

'Yes he did,' I confirmed. 'He said Preston, this is a job for someone with a criminal practice. Someone in good standing with the authorities. Try Mr. Irving Hughes.'

Hughes wasn't impatient any more. He would have been glad to listen to more of the same for another half-hour. But I couldn't spare the time.

'He told me to try you first, Mr. Hughes. But I quite understand if you don't feel able to — '

'Just a moment,' he said hastily. 'Don't think I am refusing to help. Heavens, no.'

'But I thought you said — '

'Ah, Mr. Preston, you don't realise how careful a lawyer has to be. Naturally, I wanted more information. I'll be happy to represent Mr. Delaney. Happy. Now, if you'll just let me have the details again.'

I gave him what he wanted. At the end I said:

'If you don't mind, Mr. Hughes, I'll call you later to find out what happened. Mr.

Delaney is having dinner with friends in Los Angeles this evening. I promised to call and let him know how it comes out.'

He told me to call in an hour, and I hung up. By giving Hughes the story about Delaney being out of town I'd sewn up two loopholes. In the first place he wouldn't be able to call up and check whether I was on the level. In the second, he wouldn't call to report progress and find out I'd fooled him. I was walking on very thin ice at the moment. I'd used Delaney's name to get Ventura out of jail, and he wouldn't be too well pleased when he found out. On top of that, Randall would be pretty sure where Hughes got his information about Ventura being down at Fourth Precinct. And that would put me in Dutch with the police. Pretty soon there wouldn't be anybody on my side. If I had a side. But from where I was sitting, nothing was likely to happen unless Ventura was out and around. I didn't have any real idea what the whole thing was about, but the way it stacked up, Ventura was the spark plug. Everybody else fitted, had a place in things, good or bad. Ventura was the odd ball, and so he had to be either the one making all the noise, or the cause of somebody else making it.

I drove down to the Fourth Precinct house and parked on the other side of the street. About twenty minutes went by, then a large dark-blue coupé pulled up. I knew Hughes slightly, and in the dim light I recognised his spare frame as he got out of the car and went inside. Then I settled down for a long wait. The way those things go, it wasn't too bad. After only fifteen minutes, Hughes came out again, and he wasn't alone. Beside him was the big figure of Ventura. He seemed to be wearing the same clothes as when I last saw him. At the foot of the steps they stopped. Hughes seemed to be trying to persuade the big man to get into the coupé. Whatever he was trying to sell Ventura, the other man wasn't buying. Hughes finally gave up, shrugged and got in the car. He drove off, and Ventura watched him out of sight. Then he turned and walked rapidly in the opposite direction. I let him get a good lead, then rolled the Chev after him. He went into the first phone booth he reached and made a call. I'd have given plenty to know who was on the other end. He came out of the booth and started walking again. At the next intersection, he stood on the corner, waiting. He flagged a couple of cabs, both busy. Third time he was lucky, and soon I was following the cab in and out of crosstown traffic.

It slid to a halt outside the Brown Peanut and Ventura got out. He paid the driver, but instead of going into the place he headed down an alley at the side. I got out and went after him. The Brown Peanut is an ordinary enough bar, if you want a drink. But at the rear, is one of the many offices maintained by a big-time bookmaker by the name of Lucky Hertz. It looked as though I might be about to get a break.

The alley was narrow and badly lit. It wasn't the place I'd choose to find somebody like Ventura waiting for me. But he was many yards ahead, and I let him stay that way. There were lights at the end and it seemed Ventura was to be an unannounced visitor, judging by the way he flattened himself against the wall and peered in the window. I got in on the flattening too, in case he suddenly looked round.

A long shaft of light split the gloom as a door opened, and quickly closed again. Now there was no dark shape ahead of me in the alley, and Ventura was inside. I went cautiously along the wall until I reached the window he'd been peering through. Lucky Hertz was inside, hunched over some papers, smoke from a thick cigar wreathing strange patterns around his head. As I watched he looked up, startled, and swung round. Ventura came into view and stood looking down at him. Hertz's expression was puzzled but not too concerned. Ventura said something and the bookmaker's expression changed. He made some sharp retort. The big man spoke again, hands resting on the table as he stared down with quiet hatred at Hertz. One of Lucky's hands was out of sight below the desk, and very slowly he began to inch open a drawer. It didn't need a clairvoyant to know what was inside, and I couldn't just stand there and watch murder. Everything happened at once. Lucky's hand came up fast with a big Luger in it. I shoved an elbow through the glass. Ventura gripped the table edge and tipped it forward against the bookmaker's rising arm. At the same moment he launched himself forward on top of Hertz. I was trying to reach the catch of the window. From the flurry of arms and legs on the floor of the room came a great thump of sound and then Ventura was pulling himself up, Luger in hand. He swung towards the window, a vicious snarl on his face. I yanked my arm free and dropped clear of the lighted square as the big gun went off again. Glass showered over me and a heavy slug smacked into the wall opposite. Half crouching, I began to run back towards the mouth of the alley. The .38 was in my hand now. Behind me a door slammed open. Turning I fired down the alley, and that decided Ventura against sticking his nose out. I made it to the end, ducked across the street and into the car. Inside, I sat on the floor and wound down the window, waiting for the big man to appear. There was commotion in front of the Brown Peanut now. People came out, frightened and excited, and were joined by others from the street. I ignored them, keeping my eyes glued to the narrow opening where there was a man with a gun waiting. Then there was a new sound, a mournful penetrating wail, and the blue boys were coming to take a look. It was no time for a delicate person to be out in the cold night air. I got up into the seat, roared the motor into life and got out of there fast. There were shouts as I went, and I hoped hard that the light wasn't good enough for people to pick up my plates. It was only after I rounded a corner that I became aware of pain in my arm. It was throbbing, and I could feel a familiar warm stickiness around the elbow. I pulled up and switched on the interior light. Half a dozen shards of glass were sticking out of my sleeve. It must have happened as I pulled my arm out of the window of Hertz's office. It was hurting quite a lot now, and I'd have to knock off for a repair job before I could do what I intended.

It was just one of those pieces of bad luck that always fouls things up when they seem to be working out. I'd have to go back to Parkside, and take a chance on whoever might be waiting there. It seemed to be my night for windows. First the joint on Fourteenth Street, then the Brown Peanut. Now I was going into my own apartment the same way. Emergency or no, I wasn't fool enough to go in through that big lighted entrance, remembering all the people I'd annoyed lately. I clambered up the fire escape, grunting now and again as I thoughtlessly put weight on my left arm. I got to my window and peered in at the darkness. Then I opened it, and stepped through. Feeling my way across the room, I headed straight into the bathroom without switching on lights. Inside I snapped down the switch and looked at the arm. First things first, and the first thing was to pluck out those slivers. I pulled out one, then another. There were five altogether, and I was lucky enough to get them free without breaking them. Then I peeled off my jacket and slipped out of my shirt. The damage was not too bad, five jagged cuts which would look a lot better when they'd been cleaned up and taped.

'That's quite a mess.'

I spun round to the doorway. A stocky ginger man stood looking at me, and I was relieved to see no weapon.

'What are you, a welfare worker?'

'Sort of,' he chuckled. 'I'm Jenkins. I have a badge if you want to see it.'

I shook my head. I can always tell a cop without seeing any badge.

'All right, what do you want?'

He clucked with disapproval.

'What else but you? Thought we'd take a little ride downtown.'

'What's the charge?'

'Aw c'm on Preston. What could we possibly charge you with? Just want a little talk. Captain Rourke said you'd be glad to co-operate.' He stood erect and crumpled one fist inside the other. 'And you ain't really in shape not to co-operate right this minute.'

I sighed.

'O.K. if you make sure I don't bleed to death on the way?'

'I guess it's all right. But snap it up will you?'

I snapped it up.

11

The whole committee were waiting to greet me in Rourke's office. Rourke himself, granite faced and irritable. Gil Randall, impassive and sleepy-looking. Detective First-Grade Schultz, parked on a corner chair, restless eyes flicking from one to another of us.

'Well, well boys. Look who dropped in to see us.'

Rourke's heavy sarcasm greeted me as I came through the door. The others said nothing. They knew answers are not called for when Rourke is in one of those moods.

'C'm on in Mr. Preston, and take a seat.'

I went and sat down. My arm throbbed and I put a hand to it unthinkingly.

'You notice Mr. Preston is reminding us he's hurt,' droned Rourke.

'Like to tell us how that happened, Mr. Preston?'

I didn't like either his tone or the atmosphere. This was not going to be one of those friendly occasions.

'Maybe your man did it when he came to pick me up,' I said sourly.

Rourke's face tightened.

'Are you suggesting you've been wounded by a police officer?' he demanded nastily.

'I'm not suggesting anything,' I returned defensively. 'I'm stating facts. I have fresh wounds. I have just been brought here by a police officer. I have had no medical attention. Now you don't need any outsider to tell you what a bad-minded lawyer could make of those facts, strung out in that order.'

Randall put on enough of a recognisable expression for one to tell he was puzzled.

'What is this, Preston? We have our little differences of opinion, but it isn't like you to come in here shouting lawyer. What gives?'

As the man once said, when you don't have any defense, attack. And that was what I was doing. I sneered at Randall.

'People have their own interpretations of that word 'little'. Some of those little differences we've had, I've been here all night. I can see there's something gnawing at you guys, I can smell it. And I just want you to know I won't be staying too long.'

'Hmph.'

Rourke breathed out noisy disgust and helped himself to one of his evil weeds. Those thin Spanish cigars are as much a part of the squad-room treatment as the men themselves. Sitting in a closed atmosphere for hours on end, breathing in increasing quantities of that throat-cutting smoke, has been known to assist with many investigations. Some forces hold out on the water. In Monkton they like to play tightwads with the oxygen.

Rourke exhaled the first twin funnels of air pollution and looked at the other man.

'Sergeant Randall, perhaps you wouldn't mind just running over once again what you told me a little while ago.'

Randall nodded, and began to recite in a toneless voice.

'Mr. Preston reported a murder this

afternoon. He was a material witness after the fact. Mr. Preston gave us information that meant we wanted to have a talk with one Julian Ventura. Mr. Preston warned us this Ventura was a tough character. Tonight we had a call from the Fourth Precinct. They'd picked up Ventura on another charge altogether, and they knew we were looking for him. Captain Rourke was out of the office and I couldn't get the necessary authority to have Ventura transferred here. Mr. Preston telephoned and I told him we had Ventura. Thirty minutes after that, Lawyer Hughes arrived at Fourth with a writ of habeas corpus for Julian Ventura, and got him released. Ventura made no telephone calls, and there was no other outside person but Mr. Preston who knew where he was.'

The droning ceased, and three pairs of unfriendly eyes focussed. On me.

'That's our story,' said Rourke coldly. 'What's yours?'

I tried to look nonchalant. I'd have done it better if my arm would have stopped thumping.

'Do I have a story?'

'You would be well advised to have a very good story,' Rourke told me, with emphasis. 'Because I don't like that killer being out and around the town cutting up people and so forth. It's very bad for the name of the force. It's especially bad when we had him all buttoned up and we let some smooth lawyer take him away. Some people might accuse us of being careless.'

He looked pointedly at Randall as he said that last part, and the big fellow stared at the floor.

'So that's how it stacks up Preston,' continued the captain. 'We may be in trouble for this, and I promise you one thing. The trouble we may be in will be a picnic compared to your spot. Unless there's a very lovely story. Could we hear it now?'

I chuckled, and was pleased that it didn't sound forced.

'By no means,' I refuted. 'By no means. Even if I had a story I wouldn't tell it you guys. Not in this mood. You lost Ventura, and you're looking for somebody

218

to nail up. I'm not it, better get another boy.'

'No,' said Rourke definitely. 'We like you best. Whichever way this thing turns, we always find you standing around. First there was the racetrack killing. You were there. Then this girl. You were there, too. Now this killer is loose, and that's your fault. You don't seriously imagine we're interested in anybody else?'

'I don't seriously think anything about it at all. The way it stacks up, you boys are in a jam. You, not me. And I was never one to play patsy. Besides, you take a lot for granted. We used to have a law around here about giving a man a fair trial, and a lot of sob stuff like that. I'm glad to hear you and your squad got that repealed.'

The grizzled Irishman turned a dull red around the ears.

'What is that supposed to mean? Nobody accused you of anything. Yet.'

I shook my head.

'Not talking about myself. Ventura. Every time his name comes up, you call him a killer. That kind of anticipates any trial, doesn't it?'

Schultz pulled out a knuckle with a sharp crack. Rourke looked at him irritably, and the detective stuck his hands in his pockets. Then his chief turned back to me.

'Preston, you know me better than that. I don't go around making wild statements. This Ventura is a killer. His record came through in the wire an hour ago. He already served a long term for second degree murder, and he has an assault with intent on his sheet too. Not that killing is his only little fault. He has quite a nice list. And it's only three weeks since he got out of jail up in Wisconsin on an armed robbery conviction. This guy's like an old friend.'

That didn't sit too well. To give me time to think, I dug out my Old Favorites and selected one with care. I don't know why I do that. They all look exactly the same. But what with the selecting and the lighting and inhaling, I had a few valuable seconds to make what I could out of this new information about Ventura. It certainly wasn't helping to make me feel any better about getting him out of jail.

'He sounds like a custom made suspect for all the goings-on,' I said.

'We had sort of got around to figuring that out for ourselves,' Gil Randall observed slowly. 'Now we want to know just how thick you are with this Ventura, where you fit in, and how many charges we can get you on.'

I nodded. I was beginning to wish I hadn't let them bring me in quite so easily. Outside, things could be happening. Things I could get to know about, maybe even meddle in. But that was outside, and the way things were shaping, the outside seemed to be getting further away.

'I want to make a phone call,' I said.

Rourke breathed with satisfaction and all but beamed at his men.

'Progress,' he sighed. 'And who would you call, Mr. Preston?'

'That's my business.'

'Ah yes. But that,' he tapped at the phone in front of him. 'That is my telephone. And I'm not about to let just anybody use it.'

'Don't put me on Rourke. I've been

221

around too long. A man is entitled to make one call.'

'As soon as convenient,' he reminded. 'As soon as convenient, and in any case not later than four hours after entering the station. How long has Mr. Preston been with us, boys?'

'Twenty-five minutes,' said Randall.

'Twenty-six minutes,' said Schultz.

They both spoke together, then glared at each other. Rourke chuckled.

'No matter,' he soothed. 'A small difference. Let's give him the benefit of the larger estimate. Twenty-six minutes, say. That leaves us better than three and a half hours before it has to be convenient.'

'Suit yourself,' I shrugged. 'I'll just sit here till you're ready.'

Rourke's eyes narrowed, and when he spoke his voice was dangerous.

'Preston, this I'll tell you. I don't like your line of business. I don't like people in your line of business. But in my dumb Irish way, I thought I had you figured. I thought after your own slipshod fashion, and turning a blind eye to some details of the law, you were more or less on the

222

same side as the department. I don't like people proving me wrong. If you want to play this rough, go ahead. I been a lot rougher a lot longer. So you just sit there, wait out your time, and make your phone call. Then we'll get down to business.'

I said nothing. He got up and went out of the room. Randall waited until the door was closed.

'What do you want to go and upset him for?' he demanded.

'He'll make life hell for all of us as well as you.'

'You're getting paid,' I told him.

'The sergeant is right, Preston,' cut in Schultz. 'You don't know what it's like around here when the captain gets one of his moods.'

'Look,' said Randall placatingly, 'Maybe we got off on the wrong foot. I know how Rourke says the wrong thing sometimes. People come in here, quite harmless people, and he goes and talks to them as though they were public enemies. They get offended, they clam up. Nobody gets anywhere, and the investigation suffers. I'll tell you what I think. I think the chances are you haven't done anything we couldn't overlook. I also think you know things we don't know which would help us. Now, why don't we start over? Tell us what we want to know and I'll do what I can to calm down the captain. Can't say fairer than that.'

'And he can do it, too,' was Schultz's opinion. 'I'm not saying anybody around here can fool Captain Rourke, but if there's one man has any influence with him at all, it's the sergeant here.'

They both looked at me.

'What d'you say Preston?' asked Randall.

I laughed. The air was stifling, my arm hurt, and I was in a bad mood. But I laughed.

'I'm disappointed,' I told them. 'And slightly offended. I didn't think you guys would try to work such an old-fashioned trick on me.'

'Trick?' snapped Randall.

'Trick,' I repeated. 'The nasty copper and the nice copper trick. They were doing that one back in the days of the Spanish Inquisition. I like it better when you're all nasty. This way is an offence to my professional pride.'

Randall looked at me stonily, and Schultz started cracking his knuckles again. We were still there in silence, when Rourke came back in half an hour later. He looked at each of us in turn, and sat down.

'Did he confess?' he barked.

Randall looked at his chief coolly.

'He likes us better when we're nasty,' he told him.

'Oh?' The bristly gray eyebrows raised as Rourke stared at me. 'Well, we must see we don't disappoint him.'

The telephone rang.

'Well?' Rourke almost spat into the mouthpiece. 'Well, why bother me with it? — Oh' and 'I see — The devil you say?' his voice grew more enthusiastic — 'Well of course I'm interested. Send him up here right away.'

He replaced the receiver with loving care and beamed at me.

'I've got good news for you, Preston. You are going to get your wish. In a few minutes from now we'll be in a position to get really nasty with you. That ought to make you happy.'

He was wrong. All it made me feel was apprehensive. The others were as anxious about the phone message as I was, although their reasons were different. But the captain wasn't handing out any bulletins. They were going to have to wait the same as me to find out who was coming up.

We didn't have to wait long. A shadow darkened the frosted glass on the upper half of the door, somebody knocked and the door opened. The man who put his head inside was Irving Hughes. He saw me first, bared his teeth, and then looked at Rourke.

'Captain Rourke?'

'Come in Mr, Hughes. Please come in sir. I understand you wish to file a complaint.'

The lawyer closed the door carefully. Schultz got up and placed his chair near the chief's desk for the visitor, then went and leaned against the wall. Hughes sat down, taking pains not to disturb the crease in his pants. In his neat powder blue suit, club tie and polished shoes he made the rest of us look like the night shift coming off duty. Come to think of it, we were kind of a night shift. Rourke positively exuded good humor. In Rourke's book, Hughes was O.K. and he didn't mind who knew it. Hughes was a man who enjoyed a little deference, and he was getting a fair measure from the crafty old policeman.

'I do, captain, I do.'

Rourke nodded with satisfaction, slid open a drawer and took out a pad of official looking paper. Then he picked up a thick-barreled pen and wrote something at the head of the sheet.

'All ready sir,' he glowed. 'Please tell us about it.'

Hughes pointed a forefinger at me.

'That man, Preston, deliberately gave me false information this evening which led to my securing the release of a prisoner from the custody of the police department, Fourth Precinct.'

The pen scratched. I felt Randall's eyes on me, but I didn't look at him.

'That can be a serious charge, Mr.

Hughes,' cautioned Rourke. 'Can it be substantiated?'

'It can,' replied the lawyer softly.

'Won't you describe the circumstances, please?'

'Certainly. At approximately ten-thirty this evening, I received a telephone call from this man.'

He went on with the details. What I'd said, what he said, etc.

'Mr. Hughes,' Rourke asked. 'Would you in the ordinary way accept a story like that, just on the telephone?'

'Naturally not, but this was rather different.'

'What way, different?'

Hughes looked slightly sheepish.

'For two reasons. First of all, there was this man's reputation. I'd known of him for many years naturally, and I had no idea he would be a party to such a deception with someone like myself.'

Rourke's eyebrows stuck up in the air.

'Could you make that a little clearer? Someone like yourself? Do you mean you wouldn't have been surprised to hear he'd deceived some other person?'

Hughes uncrossed his legs and smoothed out any suggestion of a wrinkle in the blue pants.

'Captain Rourke, I have a certain standing in my profession. Although I practise criminal law, I am not the type of criminal lawyer who has brought the calling into disrepute. Regrettably, there are such people, I suppose, if I can ask you not to record the remark, I suppose I would not have been surprised to hear of such an arrangement being made with a person of that type.'

'Rest assured,' said Rourke smoothly, 'That what you say here is in confidence. What you're saying is that there are other people, other lawyers around, and if Preston had contacted one of those, that wouldn't have surprised you. But with your reputation, and knowing he would know all about the way those other lawyers operate, it didn't occur to you he wasn't on the level.'

Hughes listened attentively, with his head cocked to one side in his well-known courtroom manner.

'I would never admit to saying anything

so explicit, captain. But by and large, you have the essence of it.'

'Good. Now, you said there were two reasons you thought the story was genuine. What was the other?'

'Far the more serious. Preston told me he was acting for no less a person than Mr. Clifford Delaney.'

He said it triumphantly, like a man who'd saved the ace of spades for the last trick. Rourke purred and waggled his pen around busily.

'Clifford Delaney,' he repeated smugly. 'And of course, this was not true?'

'It was not,' snapped the lawyer. 'I happened to run into Mr. Delaney quite by chance at a hotel in town half an hour ago. I mentioned to him that everything had been done as he wanted, and of course I learned the whole thing was completely unknown to him.'

Inwardly, I sighed. That's the kind of one in a million shot the gamblers dream about. The kind that people like me get nightmares about.

'Ah yes,' encouraged Rourke. 'That is very interesting. This is a very serious complaint, Mr. Hughes. And backed up by no less a person than Mr. Delaney I think we have a substantial body of evidence. Yes, what is it sergeant?'

Randall had been looking for permission to speak.

'I'd like to ask Mr. Hughes why he didn't check with Mr. Delaney before he took out the writ.'

Rourke nodded and looked at Hughes.

'The explanation was quite simple. Preston told me Mr. Delaney was out of town. Indeed, it was only my surprise at seeing he was not, that prompted me to mention the matter to Mr. Delaney when I ran into him. I confess I don't come out of this too well, captain. For a person of my calling to be duped in this way is a matter of no small embarrassment. Indeed, I may say to you that I thought very seriously of the possible damage to my reputation before I finally decided to register a complaint.'

Rourke nodded sympathetically.

'I appreciate that, sir. But you've done the right thing. In fact, you've done more than that. If you hadn't come along here,

231

and told this story, we would have had to come to you. You see, this man Ventura is not just another petty criminal. He is a killer, and we would have wanted to know why you turned him loose.'

'A killer,' repeated Hughes, and his face was ashen. 'But I had no way of knowing — '

'That's true, and I'll support that in court,' Rourke assured him. 'So far as you knew, the man was in custody on just the one charge.'

I hadn't chuckled for some time, so I chuckled.

'What's funny?' Rourke roared.

It was noticeable that his tone when he addressed me was not the same as the one Hughes was getting, but I'm not offended easily.

'I'll tell you what's funny. You are. And your lawyer buddy here. This dialogue of yours should be taped. Especially the part about agreeing to fake the evidence in court.'

I rubbed knuckles in the corner of my eye to wipe away tears of laughter. The look on Rourke's face told me he wished it was his knuckles in about the same spot.

'What was that about faked evidence,' he whispered disbelievingly.

'You'll get up in court,' I sneered. 'And who'll believe that story of yours? Didn't know the guy was a killer. You have a murder call out on him right now. Been out for hours.'

'Is that true captain?'

Hughes was less assured suddenly.

'Well, yes it is, but that's another case entirely — ' protested the Irishman.

'Just the same you have reasonable grounds for assuming this man Ventura to have committed murder?'

'Yes, if you put it that way,' admitted Rourke.

'Of course he puts it that way,' I butted in. 'He's a lawyer. He knows how lawyers think. How my lawyer will think.'

'Maybe. But that doesn't alter Mr. Hughes' position.'

'Sure it does. What have we got? He says he knew nothing about Ventura except what it said on the charge sheet. But it was me sent him down there.

Suppose I told him everything about Mr. Ventura, the whole bit? Suppose I told him Ventura had already killed once, and may be responsible for two other murders.'

'Outrageous. If I'd had the slightest inkling, the very slightest, of these other facts, I would not have acted. No, not even for Mr. Delaney.'

'But you did,' I reminded.

'In good faith. On the strength of what you told me. You know perfectly well what that was.'

I nodded and smiled at him encouragingly.

'Sure. I know, and you know. We're not talking about what the two of us know. We're talking about a courtroom, and what we might say there, and what other people will decide is the truth.'

He gnawed at his lower lip and breathed in hard. I had him on familiar ground now. The presentation of evidence, the examining and cross-examining of witnesses, months after the event.

'I see you're thinking it over, Mr.

Hughes,' I remarked.

'Not so fast,' chimed in Rourke. 'You're not forgetting Mr. Delaney, Mr. Hughes? His evidence is about on a par with that of the entire City Council.'

Hughes shook his head and made no reply.

'Mr. Delaney's evidence,' I pointed out, 'Has nothing to do with it. All Mr. Delaney can say is that he met Hughes in a hotel and Hughes asked him a question. Whatever that is worth as testimony Hughes can tell you better than I.'

'Nothing,' said Hughes sadly. 'Nothing whatever captain. Mr. Delaney knows no facts. All he could do would be to repeat hearsay, and I imagine you have some idea of the court's reaction to that.'

Rourke sighed noisily and wagged his head. I stood up.

'Well let's have it captain. Either you're going to charge Hughes and me, or I'm walking out of here.'

'You sit down,' ground Randall.

I looked at him and stayed where I was. Rourke squinted up at me.

'Charge Mr. Hughes here? What kind of a gag is that?'

'No gag. You're trying to make something of the fact that Ventura was sprung from jail. His release was obtained by a perfectly legal document. I don't know what you have in mind, conspiracy or what, but one thing is clearly established. Hughes and I did it betweeen us, and you're not going to charge me for it by myself.'

'This is nonsense.' Rourke banged the table, 'I'm not having cheap gumshoes talking to me like this in my own office.'

'Make up your mind,' I insisted. 'Are we charged or not. I'm walking out in ten seconds.'

Hughes got up and ran hands down the sides of his well-cut jacket.

'I'm sorry to be the one to say this, captain,' he observed, and it sounded as though he meant it, 'But unless there are other features, other features that will bear legal examination, this man is right. And I don't suppose you have it in mind to make any charge against me?'

Rourke waved a hand in disgust.

'No, Mr. Hughes. Certainly not. I'm satisfied, quite satisfied, that you have been bamboozled by this character. I'm also satisfied, from what you yourself said, we haven't a hope of making that stick legally.'

'Ten,' I announced.

I opened the door and walked out. Behind there was an enraged roar of 'Preston' from Rourke, but I took no notice. I went downstairs and out through the scarred doors. The night air was not cold and I breathed in deeply after the beating my lungs had taken upstairs. Then I walked over to the car and got in. The time I had lost with the homicide boys had put Ventura best part of an hour ahead of me. An hour I could ill afford. I had some visiting to do.

12

My main hope was that Ventura was guessing where to find King Ralfini, and that way it would take him a little time to locate him. I knew where to go because it was Thursday. Thursday night in Monkton is the night for the week's biggest floating crap game and I knew where the game was. I also knew the King would be there, because he never missed. Crap games are not popular with the blue boys. They find one, they close it up, toss a few people in the pokey for the night. It spoils the action, and it's also uncomfortable for those who get locked up. So the shooters have a system. They move the game around on no fixed schedule. One night it's here, another there, and it's one of the very few operations on which the police can get no advance information. So the boys are fairly certain of a few hours undisturbed play, and they pay the owner of the premises a cut off the top. Tonight the game would be at Molly's Garage, and it would just have begun to warm up.

Usually there's one mechanic doing late repair jobs at Molly's. Tonight there were three. At least there were three guys in coveralls lounging around in the semi-darkness, close by a Packard with a raised hood. In that light they'd have had difficulty in seeing whether there was any motor inside there, so it didn't seem likely they were carrying out very intricate repairs. I pulled into a vacant space and got out. The slam of the door was very loud. I'd hate anyone to think I was trying to sneak in. As I walked towards the fancy dress squad, they became suddenly quite alert.

'I'm for upstairs,' I announced.

Nobody answered. They all looked at me, then each other. One of them, a short square man, said:

'I got you. You're Preston, the private dick.'

'I don't have any cigars with me,' I told him regretfully.

One of the others spoke to the square man.

'Does he go up?'

'I guess so. Molly knows him all right. But I don't recall he ever played before.'

They were undecided.

'Private John, huh? You gonna play, or you come to make trouble for somebody up there?'

I shook my head.

'No, boys. I came to prevent trouble for all of us.' Then I remembered the square man's name. 'C'm on Mac you know me. Tell the boys it's O.K. Remember how I kept Molly out of that car-switching pinch?'

'That's right,' and he was more enthusiastic now. 'So you did. I remember. It's all right, guys. Molly thinks this guy is O.K.'

The others seemed satisfied by that.

'It's twenty bucks for in,' demanded one.

I took out some bills and counted out twenty.

'Who's playing tonight?' I queried.

The man who took the money looked at me blankly.

'We don't know any names. Just faces.'

'He knew my name,' I pointed at Mac, who grinned.

'I forgot it already.'

They moved aside to let me get to the door which led upstairs. I threaded between stacked cans of oil and up the wide stone steps. A lot of the heavy maintenance work was done on the upper floor and the cars were shifted up on a hydraulic lift. With that out of action the only way up was to use the stairs. The three phoney greasemonkeys were watching those, so the game ought to be safe enough. By the time anybody had forced his way past the guards there would have been such a commotion that the people upstairs would have plenty of warning. By the time any unwelcome visitors got up there, all they'd find would be a bunch of assorted night citizens holding a revival meeting or some such. I reached the top of the stairs. The whole of the upper floor was one big concrete spread, capable of taking twenty-five or thirty cars at one time. There were eighteen or twenty scattered around tonight. In the far corner a number of inspection lights had been hung on brackets, beams directed downwards. Under the lights a huddle of men, some kneeling some standing bent over to see the all-important cubes.

'A thousand Joe don't make it,' said an excited voice.

'I'll take half of that,' replied another.

'Gimme a hundred of what's left.'

'All right, let's cut out the noise, huh? Let the man breathe, here.'

There was an uneasy excited silence. Joe rocked back and forth, crossing gently and shaking the dice close by his ear.

'C'm on baby. Poppa got to have a lil seven. Lil ole seven. C'm on you pretty things.'

In one movement he threw the dice and snapped his fingers loudly.

'Made it. Oh, you beautiful babies. C'm on here to poppa.'

Men milled around, paying out money, taking in money, arguing. Joe began to shake his hand again, moaning softly.

'What d'you say Andy? You just spilled a grand.'

'Chicken feed,' snapped Andy. 'I got faith in this boy, Joe. He can't do it again.

Nobody's that good. Nobody.'

'Let's see the dough, Andy.'

'All right. All right. Here's two grand this time. Two. See, I'm doubling up on his luck. It has to be bad.'

The big fish took pieces of Andy's big bet. The little guys made side bets among themselves. Ten dollars, twenty. I moved between the cars studying the crowd and looking for King Ralfini. The trouble with the lighting was that coming down in narrow beams, it threw long shadows under a man's chin. If you'd told me half the guys there wore beards, I would have been in no position to argue. Then at last I saw him. He was close by the thrower, but on the outer ring of players. Slats Hooper stood beside him, hands plunged deep in his pockets. The King was following the play closely. Slats looked bored to death. While I was watching he yawned. The game went on, and I stayed where I was. By now I was satisfied Ventura was not one of the crowd. Of course he could be hidden anywhere among the cars, like I was, but I doubted that. There wouldn't be any point to it. If

243

he was going to wait for his crack at the King, then he could do that outside at a lot less risk. There weren't any windows on the upper floor, such daylight as Molly's crew was allowed finding its way through the skylight above. I looked up there, at the great rectangle of moonlit sky and all I saw was a bunch of stars reminding people there were more diverting ways of passing the time.

Although I was only twenty feet away from the excited players none of them noticed me. It was quite dark that far away from the game and a man would have to stare hard into the gloom to be able to see me. They were all far too occupied with what they were doing to spare any time for fancy staring. The King was interesting to watch. He would chuckle, and nudge Slats, then deal out green paper from the thick wad in his hand.

'Snake eyes,' came a roar.

People groaned or cheered according to which way their money was laying. Slats Hooper never removed his hands from the light topcoat. Whatever he was doing there it had nothing to do with his love for the iron men. He was there because Ralfini was there, period. I leaned against the hood of an aged Ford and wished I was home in bed. Every now and again I looked up at the stars, but that was the only exercise I was getting. My shoulder began to stiffen then my hip. It was beginning to feel cold up there, and I wanted a cigaret.

I looked for the fiftieth time at the skylight. I thought something moved. Blinking my eyes tightly I opened them for another look. There was a man's head up there, watching. I couldn't make out who it was against the sky. It was just a shape like a head. But Molly's skylight didn't carry any modern decorations. What looked like a man's head, had to be a man's head. And for my money, the head would belong to no one else but Ventura. I wasn't tired any more, not stiff. I was all lively interest now, waiting to see what happened.

The skylight moved slightly. Fully opened it would probably create a space large enough for a man to wriggle his body through. Once through, he'd have to swing around by both hands until his eyes were used to the gloom. Then he'd have to drop the greater part of fifteen feet to the floor. The King and Slats might be absorbed in the game, but that didn't make them deaf and blind. If Ventura was going to make his entrance that way, he'd have been less conspicuous leading a brass band up the stairs. It was inefficient, bungling. And what I'd seen of friend Ventura so far didn't lead me to think he'd make a fool play like that. I was right. The opening skylight stopped moving when the aperture was only inches wide. There was a dark movement against the glass. It had to be a hand, and the hand had to be holding a gun. I didn't know enough of the facts to stand around while murder was done.

'Raid,' I shouted, in panic. Then I slammed a car door. 'Raid. Break it up.'

Everybody started moving at once. Pupils distorted by the light in the playing circle, people starting to rush blindly about, bumping into cars, girders, each other. It was no place for me, and would be less so when they realised there weren't any police around. I waited until the first few reached the stairway, then slipped out of the gloom to join them. Somewhere in the crowd behind were Ralfini and Hooper, but I wasn't aiming to visit with them at that moment. We all shoved and jostled our way to the bottom where the startled Mac and the others watched in amazement. By the time the explanations began to flow the leaders were outside, and I was one of them. They started running in all directions. I made for the side alley and ducked down it. My eyes were fully adjusted to the darkness, thanks to my lonely watch at the dice game. I looked up toward the roof, and there, climbing down the rusting iron ladder at the side of the building was a large shape. It took him another ten seconds to reach bottom. As soon as his feet touched the ground I hit him across the back of the neck, and he went on folding downwards till he was just a sack of old clothes. It hadn't been a hard blow, just enough to take some of the ginger out of him while I took a little look around. Jammed in a side pocket was the Luger I'd seen Lucky Hertz pull on Ventura. It was big and it was deadly, and it had already been fired at me tonight. Holding it in my hand, I felt that quick angry fear that made me want to bend the thing around Ventura's skull. In another pocket was a spare clip of cartridges, but these were .38s and would have been useless in the Luger. He wasn't carrying anything else that would either hurt or interest me. I pushed lightly at his ribs with my foot. I pushed again, not so lightly. He groaned and put hands to his head.

'Up,' I whispered harshly. 'Up and no noise if you want to stay healthy.'

He was quick to recover. Pulling at the iron ladder he heaved himself up.

'Preston?' he queried thickly.

'Who else would let you live? We've got to move out of here, fast and light. You ready?'

By way of an answer he dived his hand into an empty pocket.

'What is it, amateur night?' I sneered. 'Do it my way, or so help me I'll ditch you and tell them where to find you.'

'Cops?'

'Not cops.' I corrected. 'Your good friend Ralfini. And his good friend Slats Hooper. You want to hear any more?'

He made up his mind quickly.

'Not now. Which way?'

I pointed, and he moved off. Outside Molly's, a group of men stood arguing. It seemed they were trying to decide who gave the phoney alarm upstairs. It also seemed they'd elected one of the heavier losers, and he didn't like the solution any too well. We were not going to make the car without being seen.

'Start singing.' I snapped.

At the same moment I clapped a loving arm around the shoulders of the startled Ventura and treated everybody to one of my rare public performances.

'Oh Adeleine-ne-ne . . . '

I always like to think I have a pleasing baritone. It pleases me well enough, when conditions are right. Ventura seemed to be a little tone deaf. He screwed up his face in distaste, and I poked a hard unfriendly finger below his ear.

'Sing.'

Now he had the message, and weighed in with a little bass work on his own account. People who sing bass the way Ventura did don't have any right to criticise others with pleasing baritones. The crowd outside Molly's seemed to agree with me.

'Shuddup,' bawled two or three.

'Go on home,' said another.

Some of the other things they said were even more pointed. But it had worked. A drunk has a special anonymity of his own. Two drunks have twice as much. They didn't know what we were doing there, and they didn't care. They just wanted us gone, and the further away the better. We made it to the car, and here I handed it to Ventura. He wanted to drive, and it took a minute of drunken argument to persuade him into the passenger's seat. Thankfully I climbed in behind the wheel and roared the motor.

'Where we going?' demanded the big man.

'Friend of mine,' I explained. 'My place is no good. Your buddy Ralfini has already sent clowns there before.'

'Don't call him my buddy,' he growled.

After that there was no more talk. I headed for 14th Street. The place looked even more unprepossessing in the middle of the night than it had earlier. So did the old coot who probably called himself the night manager.

'Anybody asking after me?' I demanded.

'Nossir,' he said quickly. 'Things are real quiet tonight.'

'Anyone gets up those stairs, things'll get noisy,' I assured him. 'Here.'

I put a ten on the counter. Dirty fingers clawed at it. Ventura watched the performance in silence.

'I got you,' protested the old man. 'No visitors.'

We went upstairs and I knocked at the room where I'd left Thompson.

'Just a minute,' he called from inside.

We waited, then there was a chuckle behind us. We swung around to find Thompson standing there. He'd used the connecting door between the room then let himself out in the corridor. That way he could take a good look at his visitors.

'Inside,' I nodded.

We all trooped in. Thompson looked at Ventura enquiringly, but asked no questions.

'This is the guy who owns the room,' I explained.

Ventura glowered at the pair of us.

'What's this with the room?' he demanded. 'I don't own no rooms.'

'Wrong,' I corrected. 'You own this one. For tonight anyway. And the one next door.'

He puzzled it through.

'You mean you took these rooms in my name? What kinda play is that?'

I shrugged.

'Well, as it turns out, a pretty dumb idea. I thought there might be people looking for you. I also thought I'd like to meet those people. So I booked into the joint in your name, and left my friend here to see if anybody came around.'

'And nobody did,' supplied Thompson.

Ventura was not reassured.

'Not yet they didn't. Anyways, before it didn't matter. Before there was only his head to blow off. Now I really am here.

252

With my own name in the register I might as well hang up a sign.'

'Relax,' I told him, 'There's three of us. If anybody shows it'll only be one guy, maybe two. It takes a lot of people to cover a town this size.'

'I'm getting outa here,' decided Ventura.

Thompson moved easily in front of the door. I clicked my tongue in annoyance.

'Now look,' I said wearily. 'Don't let's have one of these sessions where I have to keep waving the gun. You know I have it, so why don't you behave?'

The big man hesitated, measuring up Thompson, weighing his chances in a brawl with the two of us. Then he sighed.

'Ah, what the hell. I'm played out anyway. Is there a drink?'

I nodded to Sam who went next door, and came back with a bottle and a chipped tumbler.

'Never mind the glass.'

Ventura took the bottle, caressed it fleetingly, then shoved the open neck into his mouth. He took a deep draught, shuddered and sighed.

'O.K.' he said softly, almost musingly. 'O.K. Preston.'

When he was through with his second swallow, the bottle had taken a bad beating.

'That's better. That is better.'

Thompson reached out for the bottle. Ventura thought about hanging on to it, then released it with a brittle laugh.

'Now we talk, Ventura.'

'Talk? I got nothin' to talk about,' he said dreamily.

'You're too modest,' I informed him. 'We are going to talk. As you said, you're about played out. But I'm still in the game. Better let me see your cards if you want this thing to work out your way.'

'My way?' he scoffed. 'Oh sure, you and me, we're big buddies.'

'No,' I corrected. 'I don't like you a bit. But I think you may be doing the right thing for once in your life. Pity to let it get away from you, just because you're too stupid to see sense.'

He made a sucking noise between his teeth.

'You say there's two rooms?'

'That's right.'

'Why don't your partner here go watch the other one? In case they sneak up on us from behind? And he could leave the booze.'

Thompson looked at me. I nodded.

'Do it, Sam.'

'And shut the door,' added Ventura.

When we were alone, he looked over at me.

'It's your party, brother. You sing first.'

'All right. I'll tell you what I know, add in a few pieces I think I know. You fill up any spaces. O.K.?'

'We'll see. It depends what you got.'

I hadn't anything to lose.

'O.K. You call yourself Ventura these days. You weren't always Ventura. Once upon a time you were an actor, small-time vaudeville mostly. Tapper Holland. You worked a double with your wife. Tapper Holland and Molly. Molly started playing around, and you killed her. There was a daughter then, just a small baby at the time. The law put you away, and you went bad. When you came out you became a regular stick-up artist. The daughter got adopted. You didn't want to claim her back, but you liked to keep an eye on her, find out how she was getting along. You had this friend, Race Rendell. Once a year he'd get down this way for the meeting. While he was here he'd find out how your daughter was getting along, then report to you next time he saw you. How'm I doing?'

'Keep talking,' he grunted.

'This year, a month or two back, Race didn't have a very good story. The daughter was due to get married, and that was O.K. That was fine. But something else wasn't so fine. The man who adopted her, the man she thought was her father, he was keeping very bad company. Playing a regular card game with professionals, and losing every week. That looked like what it was, blackmail. A nice painless and untraceable blackmail, performed right out in the open. You knew these monkeys had got the story about your daughter — say how did you know that, by the way?'

'Just finish the story.'

'Nothing more to it. You decided to put

them out of business. Race helping you. Race got killed, now it's just you and them. End of story.'

'You're wrong,' he contradicted. 'We didn't get to the end yet. Still, I gotta admit, you figure pretty good.'

'Tell me some of the bits I don't know,' I suggested.

'What for? You know I have to finish you too. Otherwise the chances are you'll take up with Lishman where these other guys left off.'

'Crazy,' I told him. 'I don't work that way. And anybody here in town will tell you so. Don't be so dumb, Ventura. I'm the nearest thing you'll get to a friend.'

He grinned wolfishly.

'I'm kinda choosy about my friends.'

I pushed an Old Favorite in my face and sighed.

'You can play this any way you want. Just about everybody in town is looking for you by this time. King Ralfini has probably put the word out on you. That means every chiseller within miles can get close to a soft dollar just by making a phone call.'

'The word's been out before. I'm still around,' he boasted.

'Plus,' I went on. 'The law boys are very anxious to get you back in custody. And this time they'll keep you. They may even keep you for ever, after that Hertz thing.'

He stiffened slightly.

'Hertz thing?'

'Sure. You remember. You knocked him off an hour or two back.'

'You're crazy.'

'Not so. I was the one out in the alley, you almost blew off my head.'

'It's a real big shame I didn't.'

But he was a shade less confident than previously.

'That's the way it stacks up,' I continued. 'You have every no-hoper in town plus every police officer, all on the other side of the fence. You may have a big opinion of yourself, Ventura, but you're not so good you can beat those odds.'

He tapped at his knees with thick fingers.

'It was Race's idea to get you in this,' he muttered. 'All you done so far is steal my roll and get in the way. Let me ask you something.'

'Go ahead.'

'You cleaned me out. Took most of five grand off me. I don't have any more, and you don't even think I have.'

'So?'

'So why do you stick around unless it's to put the bite on Lishman? There's no other gravy in this stew except the Lishman gravy.'

I dropped ash on the floor, ground it underfoot.

'I've been hired to poke around.'

'Ah,' his eyes gleamed. 'And who is the hiring boss?'

'Friend of Race's. The same guy told Race to get in touch with me.'

'Him? The wop? What's the name — er — '

'Lugio, Johnny Lugio. And don't call him a wop.'

'Sure that's him, Lugio. A square little guy. But he can't afford to hire people like you. I know you guys, bloodsuckers. Lugio couldn't meet your bar bills.'

'Ask him,' I returned. 'He hired me.

And ask yourself this. The whole mess started because you wanted something done. You wanted to keep your daughter and the rest of the world from hearing the story. That's how it started. Now we have people getting killed, maybe more to come. The thing has changed into a private war between you and Ralfini. The chances are he's going to win. All the odds are in his favor. But the important thing is, if he wins this one, he wins the whole game. He'll go on bleeding Lishman dry, and in the end maybe the whole story will come out anyway. It could happen. So we'd have Race dead, Arabella dead, Hertz dead, maybe you too. We'd have Francis O. Lishman busted, and all for nothing. All for absolutely nothing, because the girl finds out anyhow. Kind of funny, really. Think about it.'

Ventura scowled and rubbed a huge hand across his eyes wearily.

'You saw what they did to Belle?' he demanded.

'I saw,' I nodded.

'Somebody's gonna pay for that.'

'Somebody named Slats Hooper?' I hazarded.

'Sure. It was Slats all right. I know that lousy creep. Know the way he operates. He'd have liked that just fine.'

'The police have an idea you might have done it,' I said gently.

His face was outraged.

'Me?' he spluttered. 'Me pull a thing like that? You watch your mouth peeper, or I'll spread it round the walls.'

For a moment it looked as though he might do just that. He was big enough. I eased out the .38 and let it lie on my lap. That way I felt more comfortable.

'So you knew Slats before?' I asked.

'Ah, what's the diff? May as well tell you. Him and me, we was in stir together. He was near the end of a four-year term, they had him working in the hospital. I got me a little still running in the workshop, turning out a few jugs of alkie. One batch we made up from some wood polish. It went bad on us, and I wound up on a stretcher. I was pretty sick for a couple of days, and I must have talked my fool head off.'

'So that's how Slats got to know the set-up here in Monkton,' I mused.

'Sure. He ain't dumb, that Slats. I'll say that for him. He could see his way to a nice little spot with the local big fish.'

'Why not go straight to Lishman himself, scoop the whole pot?' I questioned.

'Nah. That would be dumb. That way a guy could get in trouble. What Slats did was the wise thing. He cuts in the big boys, everybody loves him.'

'It struck me as very lucky for Slats that Ralfini's bodyguard happened to get himself beaten up just around the time Slats was looking for work.'

'There wasn't no luck about it. Slats fixed that personal.'

'But why would Ralfini hire him? Come to that, why should he even believe the story?'

Ventura looked at me pityingly.

'Why wouldn't he? Slats had the proof, all those papers he stole offa me back there in the pen.'

'Ah. You didn't tell me that part. Well, if Slats had them, how come Race had them

262

stacked away at the express office?'

The big man snorted with exasperation.

'I woulda thought you was smart enough to figure all this. Slats had the stuff, and him and the others knew about it. O.K?'

'O.K.'

'So we got two problems. One, we gotta get back my papers. That's the evidence, and anybody can use it. Two, we gotta take care of those guys who know what's in the package. That way we clean up the whole mess.'

'So Race managed to get hold of the stuff,' I supplied.

'Yeah. But he was unlucky. Slats saw him as he was leaving the place. He knew he was some track bum by the clothes. All he had to do was police the track next day until Race showed.'

'I see. But how did it come about that you left Race unprotected? You would have known what Slats and the others would do to him, once they caught up.'

A shadow passed across the heavy face.

'That is a bad spot you're kicking. We

had this deal. If Race got away with the papers, he'd bring them to me at Belle's place. If there was trouble, he'd keep away and we'd meet up later at the track.'

'He didn't want to lead the trouble boys to your doorstep, was that the way it went?'

'Sure, naturally. That way I'd still be out and around. Race got himself in any trouble, there'd still be me to do something about it.'

A thought struck me.

'But you told me you saw him put the package in the express company box. How could you do that if you weren't with him?'

Ventura looked at me with cold eyes.

'He had to take a chance. You forced him to do that.'

'I did?'

'Sure. We had your name from this guy — er — Lugio. But he couldn't raise you at your office. He called me up on the phone. Said he'd park the papers in the box till he could find you. He had me send Belle down to the company office. She didn't talk to Race, just watched where he put it, then came back to put me wise. You know the rest of it.'

'All but the most important part,' I contradicted.

'Yeah? What's that?'

'The end. Stories have to have an end.'

He looked at me with something like pity.

'You're pretty dumb, aincha? The end is easy. I knock off Slats, then this Ralfini, just to be safe. Then I blow.'

Slowly, I shook my head.

'Sorry, Ventura. I understand what you're doing, and I think I understand why, but no soap. I can't let you loose on the town.'

He sneered.

'What's your program? I stay here till I die of old age?'

'There's always the police,' I reminded.

He laughed then, a short rasping sound.

'You're crazy, as well as dumb. I'll tell the cops you were in on the whole thing from the start. You'll get ten years, maybe more.'

He was probably right. I was trying not to think that far ahead.

'I'll just take my chances.'

The big man stared at me, as though trying to make up his mind about something.

'Lugio was right about you. You really are on the level. You want a shot of this before I empty the bottle?'

I shook my head. He tipped the bottle expertly against his lips and began to swallow greedily. I say he began to. Next thing I knew the half full bottle was flying at my head. I pulled sideways and grabbed for the gun. The bottle hit me about half a second before Ventura. It grazed the side of my temple hard, just as Ventura's powerful arm chopped down on my shoulder. The gun slid off my lap. I rolled to the floor after it and just managed to wedge my hand under a huge crushing foot.

'Take it easy,' he advised.

The .38 was in his hand as the adjoining door swung open and Thompson hurtled in.

'Hold it right there,' snapped Ventura, and there was something in his voice that pulled Sam up short.

I nursed my bruised hand and sat upright. The room kept on advancing at me, then receding, with alternate thumps from the swelling egg on the side of my head.

'Now what?' I croaked.

'Now we come to the end of that story you was talking about.'

'What are you going to do with us?' I demanded.

'Nothing,' he returned. 'I got no reason to knock you off, or your little brother here. I think you levelled with me. But don't get in the way of what I'm gonna do, Preston. Anybody in the way has to get this, understand?'

He patted at the gun.

'You won't get one half mile,' I told him.

'Maybe. Whatever comes outa this, you keep quiet about what you know. Funny thing, I almost trust you.'

He backed to the door. I shook a warning head at Sam Thompson who seemed to be working up for a try at the gun. Ventura snorted with satisfaction and opened the door behind him.

'Get some shut-eye,' he advised. Then he was gone.

Thompson looked at me.

'Well?' he demanded.

'Well what?'

'Do we go after him, put the police onto him or what?'

'Nothing. We sit around and smoke awhile. Then we go pay a call.'

He looked and sounded bewildered.

'This ain't like you. Suddenly you're a do-nothing character? It ain't like you at all.'

'I'm not just doing nothing,' I denied. 'I'm waiting.'

'Waiting for what?'

I tossed him a cigaret and lit one myself.

'Sort of like a chef,' I explained. 'I get the ingredients, prepare them, mix them up. Finally they go on the stove. What does the chef do then?'

'I guess he stands around and waits for whatever he's cooking up.'

'That's a very good guess,' I nodded. 'That is exactly what old chef Preston is doing right this minute.'

He wagged his head uncertainly, then lowered himself into a chair. 'Hope you know what you're doing. That guy is about to kill somebody. You heard what he said.'

I didn't want to think about that. It didn't make it any easier for me just sitting around. Thompson was right. I never would have made a chef.

'Come on,' I decided.

Now he was really puzzled.

'What happened to the waiting?' he demanded.

'I got a better idea. Besides, we don't want this pie to burn.'

13

Downstairs in the lobby there was no sign of the old man. There was a small telephone switchboard behind the desk that must have created a lot of excitement among the cowhands when it was first installed. I fooled around with plugs and aged pieces of wire till I finally contacted someone in the outside world. I gave the number and waited. It was a long wait.

'Who's going to answer at this hour? It's almost four in the morning,' complained Thompson.

'Then somebody will just have to get out of bed,' I told him.

It was more than ten minutes before I got an answer. The voice at the other end was not friendly.

'Well?'

'Mr. Lishman? This is Preston.'

'Who?'

I explained who I was, and he remembered.

'Do you know what time it is?' he exploded. 'What is it that can't wait till morning?'

'I need to see you right now, Mr. Lishman. The morning is too far away. You know what it's about, and you'll have to take my word it's necessary.'

He forgot he was tired and bad-tempered.

'Where?'

'Corner of Laketree Drive. Fifteen minutes too soon?'

'I can make it. Will I need anything? Like money for instance?'

He wasn't cracking at me. It was a genuine question.

'Any spare cash you can roust up may come in handy. Can you run to a thousand?'

'Do my best. Fifteen minutes.'

He hung up. Thompson leaned on the stained counter.

'I give up. I quit,' he said helplessly. 'Who is this guy we bite for a thousand bucks in the middle of the night?'

'Never mind that now. We have fourteen minutes to get there.'

We went out into the deserted street and climbed into the Chev.

'Is there going to be any trouble, like shooting trouble?' asked Thompson.

I sped along the dark canyons of the city, hoping no over anxious policeman would get inquisitive.

'Could be,' I replied.

'Great. What do we do, show 'em our muscles?'

I took out the Luger and passed it to him. He sighed with satisfaction.

'Well now, this is better. This is a whole lot better.'

'Check the clip Sam. Ventura's been making war with that thing already.'

He fiddled around in the darkness, then held the clip by the side window, catching the faint light that came in.

'Let me off at the next stop, conductor,' he asked. 'There are exactly two items of any value in this firing piece. Where I come from that ain't enough.'

It certainly wasn't any great encouragement.

'It'll be good training,' I told him. 'We just hadn't better miss anybody.'

'Hey, maybe the guy with the all-night bank will bring a little something with him, huh?'

'Maybe.'

We made it to Laketree Drive with one minute to spare. There was no other parked car on view. I killed the lights and we sat waiting.

'As you know, I have a reputation as a man who never asks any questions,' intoned my passenger. 'But just this one time I am going to break a rule. Where are we going, and what are we going to do when we get there? And furthermore, who will be in charge of the artillery?'

'In a minute Sam. I don't want to have to tell it all twice. Ah, that might be him now.'

A long black shape slid around the corner, headlights blazing. The car rolled smoothly towards us, parking in front. Lishman got out and walked towards us. He was wearing a topcoat, and one hand was jammed significantly in a pocket.

'He's got one too,' whispered Sam. 'He won't point it at the wrong people will he?'

'Stay here Sam, I'm going to talk to him.'

'You said I could listen.'

'Not to the first part.'

I got out. Lishman stood watching me, like a man who was expecting trouble. He looked even broader than when I last saw him.

'That's close enough,' he snapped. 'Let's hear the story.'

'Did you manage to find any money?' I countered.

'All I could scrape together with a little over seven hundred dollars. And you don't get that until I know what this is all about.'

'I don't want it,' I returned. 'It's carfare for someone leaving town.'

'I'm waiting.'

He was on edge. I hoped he wasn't one of those people who get twitches in the fingers when upset. Because unless I was very much mistaken, Lishman's fingers were curled around something in the coat pocket. Something with a butt at one end and a hole in the other. The hole would be pointing at the general direction of my middle, which didn't need any holes today.

'Last time we talked you never heard of anybody named Ventura,' I reminded him. 'Has the situation changed?'

'Who is that sitting in your car?' he evaded.

'Friend of mine. And his name isn't Ventura.'

'I — may have heard of the man.'

'The people who may have mentioned him would be your great card-session buddies?'

'Perhaps.'

'And just what did they tell you about him?'

'He's another one of the same breed. You seem to know what this is all about.'

'I know about your daughter, I know about the card game and what it's costing you. I know most of it, maybe not all. The first time I came to see you, you thought I had a ticket on the gravy train. You were wrong.'

'I'm sorry,' he said stiffly. 'But you can understand my position, since you know so much. From what I was told, you were going to be another mouth to feed if I couldn't get you away from my affairs.'

'I don't get my vitamins that way,' I said nastily. 'Is that what they told you about Ventura too?'

'More or less.' He moved aside slightly so that he could get a better view of Thompson in the car. 'They said this Ventura wanted them out of the way so he could take over from them.'

'And you never heard of Ventura before?'

'Never.'

I thought I believed him, but it would have helped if I could have seen his face clearly.

'Let's try another key,' I suggested. 'This guy wasn't always Ventura. A long time ago he used to have another name. He was in vaudeville then, he and his wife.'

'No,' he said thickly. 'No, I don't believe you. It can't be, not after all these years.'

'Yes it can,' I pressed on. 'Do you think you might have known him by another name?'

Lishman nodded.

'If the name was Holland.'

'That's the one.'

'But I thought he was dead. I mean, all these years and never a word from him. Now you say he's here in Monkton City, involving himself in things again. I would be the first one he'd contact. I mean he wouldn't need to get involved with Ralfini and the rest. They only know things, hold documents. He is the living proof. Why doesn't he get on to me direct?'

He was talking as much to himself as to me. His voice had a faraway quality, and there was no doubt the presence of Holland on the scene was news to Francis O. Lishman.

'Because they fed you a yarn,' I told him. 'Holland or Ventura, call him what you will, he doesn't want your money. He's here in town for one reason only, to get those guys off your back and keep the girl from finding out the truth about her father.'

It still hadn't fully registered.

'To — to stop those men?' he queried faintly.

'That's it. The man is a criminal and he knows how these things go. If you could pay, and that would be the end of it, he'd most likely leave you to it. But blackmail never works that way. Sooner or later something would happen. If you couldn't pay any more they'd talk, and it would all come out. Or you may get so you could no longer stand it, and run amok with a gun. That would bring it all out too. So Ventura worked it out, the only way to close up a deal of this kind in his way. And that's what he's doing.'

'But they'll kill him.'

'Probably. But he's doing all right so far. He got rid of Hertz a few hours ago. Now he's out looking for Ralfini and Slats Hooper. He could get lucky.'

'I see. And you. What has any of it to do with you?'

There was no suspicion in the enquiry now. After the bombshell about Ventura being Holland, there was nothing I could say that would surprise Lishman in the slightest.

'I was hired by a little guy to sort of poke around. I didn't know quite what I was getting into. There'll be no check.'

Lishman didn't even ask who was paying me. He said:

'And now you want me down here at this hour with cash. Is it to help Holland get away?'

'I couldn't suggest that to you Mr. Lishman, and I won't. The man is wanted by the police. I operate under a license issued by the State of California, and people like me don't help criminals to dodge the net. If we catch up with him at all, what you do with your money is your business.'

'I think I have your meaning. I brought a gun.'

He didn't say that he brought it in case he needed it to deal with me. That was in the past. The new aim would be to use it to help Ventura if the chance came his way.

'Keep it in your pocket, and keep your hands away from it,' I advised.

'This isn't your kind of play, Mr. Lishman. If I need the help I'll holler, and fast. But don't go shooting off any guns unless its vital. Remember, a few questions from the police and this whole mess will break wide open.'

'But it's my mess,' he protested. 'None of you would need to be in this but for me. Besides, I have to think of my daughter.'

'Do that,' I agreed. 'Just keep that little thought planted right in the front of your mind. The whole deal is to keep her from knowing things. Every action should be conditioned to that fact.'

'You're right of course. Just makes a man feel so damned useless.'

'We may still be glad of the gun,' I consoled. 'The next move is to find Ventura.'

'Very well. Have you any idea where to start?'

'Yup. We get to where the others are, and we'll find him.'

'Won't they be home in bed? It's almost five in the morning.'

I grinned in the darkness.

'No, Mr. Lishman, they will not be in bed. They are night people. That doesn't mean just that they go to bed late. They have a different rhythm altogether. They don't get up till afternoon and they get to bed between six and seven in the a.m. There are two places in town where the night people start to gather for breakfast about now. One is Mac's Bar and Grill, the other is Sooty Weldon's place out at the Bluffs.'

'Which one do you think they'll use?'

'We'll try Mac first. Keep about thirty forty yards behind me on the road.'

I got back into the Chev. Thompson yawned.

'What was that all about? You took your time.'

'We have to find some people,' I replied. 'I'm trying Mac's first.'

'Ah me. Well at least we'll get decent java. Mac bakes the best in town.'

I didn't want Ralfini to be at Mac's. Ventura hadn't a car, and at that hour of the morning it would take a while to locate a cab. But Mac's was only a twenty minute walk away from the joint on Fourteenth Street. Ventura could easily have made it there by this time and butchered half the customers. The other place out at the Bluffs, was a different proposition. It was eight miles from town, and not every hackie would jump for joy at the prospect of carrying a fare who looked like Ventura that far out into the night.

I pulled in opposite the diner and waited till Lishman snapped off his lights behind me.

'He's had plenty of time to get this far,' I told Thompson. 'I'll just poke my head round the door. If he's here we'll know quick enough.'

Motioning Lishman to stay where he was, I walked across the street and opened the door of Mac's. A rush of stale warmth and fresh coffee hit me in the face. Behind the scrubbed counter Mac looked at me without interest. When you've been an all-nighter as long as Mac, you gave up being interested in anything years ago. I went inside and leaned towards him confidentially.

'Have you seen Ralfini or Hooper?' I muttered.

'I gotcha. Preston, the man with the nose. I don't know those people,' he told me throatily.

'Mac, be smart for once. I have to find those guys and quick. The King is about to catch a lot of trouble if I don't find him. He won't think you're a very nice guy if you couldn't be bothered to help him.'

Mac nodded, and picked thoughtfully at a rear tooth.

'Level?'

'You heard me.'

'He ain't coming today. There's some action some place the other end of town. When he goes there, he gives me a miss. Could find him at Sooty Weldon's, maybe. What kinda trouble?'

'So long, Mac.'

A tired blonde at the end of the counter was straining her ears trying to pick up the dialogue. When she saw me looking at her she stirred furiously at the cup in front of her. I went out.

'Nothing,' I told Thompson. 'He has to be at the next stop, or we're lost.'

I made road out to the Bluffs. The sky was yawning now, clouds scratching themselves sleepily, and here and there the faint light of early day pierced the gloom.

'I oughta be home in bed,' grumbled Thompson.

'People die in bed,' I said automatically.

'People could be dying where we're going, too,' he replied.

I dug the pedal into the floor. Sooty Weldon likes to think his place has a little tone. It snuggles in a thick bank of tall trees, which certainly keeps it private. The overhead foliage wasn't ready to let any daylight through yet as we rolled towards the big wooden structure. There were several cars outside.

I parked just short of the building and climbed out. Sam got out too, stretching and making tired noises. Lishman pulled in behind the Chev, cut the motor and got out.

'What now?' he demanded.

'I don't know,' I confessed. 'First thing is to find out whether those guys are in there.'

'Maybe our boy already made his play,' suggested Thompson.

'No,' I decided. 'If he'd started, the place would be alive with cops and newspaper guys. We have to know whether the others are here.'

We walked towards the lights. Lishman came too.

'Not you,' I told him. 'You are here for emergencies only. And as cashier if there's a chance of getting Ventura away.'

'There won't be.'

It wasn't Lishman's voice. It wasn't Thompson's either. It came from a nearby cedar tree. As I was puzzling about this, the tree chuckled, and from behind it stepped a man. There was just enough light to reflect dully on the stutter-gun cradled in his arms.

'I oughta knock you off right now,' he snarled.

'Oh no,' I said confidentially. 'Ventura, yes. But not us.'

'Don't take any bets,' he snarled.

'Not us,' I repeated. 'Not in front of Mr. Lishman. He's your meal-ticket Slats. Kill us with him looking, and you might as well tear up the ticket.'

'I don't get it,' objected Thompson.

'You see Sam, Slats here and his buddy Ralflini, they have a little blackmail going. Mr. Lishman is the beneficiary as you might say.'

'And?'

'And if little Slats here does blow our heads off — you'd like that wouldn't you Slats — '

'I'd love it,' he ground out. 'And don't you push too hard — '

' — If he does,' I continued, — 'why, then Mr. Lishman will make a lovely murder witness. And he'd love *that*.'

'You're absolutely right, Preston,' said Lishman.

To do him justice, I couldn't hear his teeth chattering at all. I wished I was as confident as I sounded.

'So we have a stand-off, you see Sam?'

Thompson grunted. All he could see was a large submachine gun held by a man who knew where the trigger was. A man who'd used one before.

'If it's that easy,' he queried, 'why don't we just take that thing away from him?'

Hooper shifted, and arced the hand grip towards us.

'Come and try,' he encouraged.

Nobody rushed forward.

'No, Sam, we can't do that,' I regretted.

'Because he wouldn't mind just cutting off our feet with it, or some little thing like that. He doesn't want to, because of Mr. Lishman. But he wouldn't mind.'

'I'd love it, baby. Come and try me.'

Hooper was breathing quickly, and I knew if we pushed too hard he'd let himself go, Lishman or no. A car headlights showed in the distance.

'Here's our little buddy now,' snapped Hooper. 'Back outa sight, the lot of you. You too, Lishman. Don't think I'm kidding with this little sweetheart.'

'Do as he says,' I ordered.

We pressed back beneath the trees as the lights came nearer. Hooper began to whistle, a high off-key sound that pierced unhappily through the soft sighing of the trees. He was behind us, and I knew if any of us made a move he'd cut us down like ripe corn. I hoped Lishman wouldn't decide to go for hero. The car drew nearer and we all held our breath. Hooper's tuneless pipe ceased, and I got ready to fling myself out of range. An aged Buick came along the narrow road. The interior light was on, and a young fair-haired character drove slowly by, eyes fixed on the lights ahead. I was close enough to see there was no-one else in the car. Hooper chuckled.

'I'd like to seen the kid's face if he knew what he just passed.'

I had an idea.

'Is it always this way, Hooper? You do all the rough work while your pal Ralfini sits in the warm and waits?'

Hooper chuckled.

'Oh brother. Where did you pick up this rusty technique? What am I supposed to do, get sore and throw in with you guys? Besides, you don't need to worry about the King. Look over there.'

I peered into the darkness. Branches moved suddenly and became Ralfini. The fat man chuckled.

'I don't like too much publicity,' he purred, 'I thought I'd kind of let Slats have the limelight. If you people tried to give him a bad time, I could kind of help out from over here.'

There was something in his hand, the kind of something people need when they're out on a dark road waiting for a man with a gun. The Buick door banged and we all jumped nervously towards the sound. The blonde boy got out and ran up the steps into Weldons, two at a time.

'False alarm,' grunted Ralfini. 'Maybe next time.'

We waited ten minutes, fifteen. Lishman shivered in his topcoat. I didn't have one, and I was doing plenty of shivering too. Then there were more lights coming, two cars at least, maybe three.

'Back up,' ordered Ralfini. 'Looks like we're going to have a party.'

We were all straining our eyes at the coming lights. I didn't see how it could be Ventura. The guy didn't need a motorcade to get him here. I heard the sound of a breaking twig behind me. At the same instant a gun roared. Ralfini screamed and clawed at his chest. I dropped to the ground fast, shoving Lishman as I went. Hooper roared with rage as he swung the deadly chopper in the direction of the shot. Heavy lead pumped into the darkness in a half-circle, and a man cried in pain. Hooper laughed excitedly.

'C'm on punk. Come and git some more.'

Again the hammering began and again came a choked cry. Beside me Lishman suddenly pulled a hand from his pocket. There was an old-fashioned peace officer's revolver in his hand. Rolling on his back he sighted it at Hooper, who was turned half away.

'No,' I shouted, but too late.

The revolver barked once, twice. Both slugs went into Hooper's side. He coughed and let the sub-machine gun drop from his hands. His knees began to sag as he turned towards the man who'd shot him.

'Some day,' he croaked, 'I'll get you for — '

Then he fell forward on his face. He was dead before he hit the ground. I snatched up the Thompson and ran to Ralfini. He was dying fast, and wasn't going to hurt anybody. A bulky figure loomed out of the darkness, pulling himself along by the dangling branches.

'Where did he get you, Ventura?' I shouted.

He peered hazily around.

'Lishman, gimme the gun.'

Lishman was on his feet now, staring down in horror at what had once been Slats Hooper. At the sound of Ventura's voice, he took a step away, ready to use the revolver again if he had to. Ventura waved feebly.

'Gimme — ' was all he could manage.

He wasn't holding my .38. It must have dropped out of his hand back in the bushes. I understood then.

'Give it to him,' I snapped urgently.

Lishman didn't get it. The lights from the approaching cars were getting very close. Impatiently I stepped across and snatched the gun from his hand.

'Here.'

I pressed it into Ventura's outstretched palm. He grinned.

'You know, you're nearly half smart. We coulda — '

Then an expression of terrible agony came on his face and he coughed blood. Cars were stopping all around, search-lights picking out the scene.

'You have two seconds to drop that,' shouted a voice.

Realising suddenly he was talking to me, I dropped the Thompson which had become red-hot. To Lishman I hissed:

'Ventura shot Hooper. Remember it.'

There was no time for any more. They were everywhere, men in faded khaki uniforms with guns and questions. They had hard suspicious eyes that wanted me to grab for the machine-gun so they could cut me down.

'Well well. Two dead and one more in a couple of minutes. You had yourself quite a time with that thing.'

A surly looking man with a county sheriff's badge stared into my face.

'You're crazy,' I said wearily. 'How'd you get out here anyway?'

'Little bird.'

The sheriff looked at Lishman. Maybe the topcoat made him different from the rest of us.

'You the guy sent the message?' he demanded.

'Message?' queried Lishman blankly.

'Sure. We got a message there was

going to be a war out here. Guy said he brought out some hoodlum in the luggage compartment. The hood said to park outside Weldon's, beat it and phone the law. Not you, huh?'

Lishman shook his head, so did Thompson. The sheriff didn't even look at me. Guys who use machine-guns don't holler for the law.

'This one's talking, Sheriff.'

A man crouched beside Ventura called over his shoulder. The sheriff looked down.

'How many did I get?' muttered Ventura.

'What's he saying?' snapped the sheriff.

'Sounded like 'How many did I get?' ' replied the kneeling man.

'You got two, Ventura,' I shouted. 'You killed two of us.'

Ventura coughed, and more blood ran from his mouth.

'That's too bad,' he whispered. 'I oughta — '

Then his head snapped sideways. The sheriff looked at him, then at me.

'You heard him, Sheriff,' Sam Thompson chipped in. 'Can I go home now?'

'Try it, and you'll go home in a box. What are you grinning at?'

'Me?' I denied. 'I'm just hoping maybe I'll get a ride out to your nice county headquarters.'

'You got your wish, loudmouth.'

'Well you won't want him,' I pointed at Lishman. 'He was just trying to get past when Hooper stopped the car and made him get out.'

'Hooper? Who's Hooper? You mean Slats Hooper?'

'That's who I mean,' I confirmed. 'Slats threw a chopper at this man and made him get out. He's that passing stranger you always hear about. Isn't that right mister?'

I looked hard at Lishman, to be sure he had it right. He pursed his lips, for a moment I thought he was going to start an argument. Then, very slowly, he nodded.

'That's right, Sheriff. I don't know any of this riff-raff. I am Francis O. Lishman, of the F.O.L. Construction Company. Everyone in Monkton City knows who I am.'

The sheriff stared at him thoughtfully, then back at me.

'Respectable citizen huh, Mr. Lishman?'

'Completely. You needn't take my word. You may refer to anyone you choose.'

Lishman was very stiff and starchy, like any good citizen dragged into a mess. I hoped he could keep it up. The sheriff was smarter than he appeared.

'Well, O.K. Mr. Lishman. Now, you can see the jam I'm in here. This is a real mess, and I'll be glad of your cooperation in helping me get it straightened out.'

'Certainly. Anything I can do, of course. But I hope it won't take too long, Sheriff. This has been a terrible experience.'

'I understand. I'll make it as fast as possible.'

The sheriff turned away and began barking orders. From the side of my mouth I hissed.

'Tell everything exactly as it was after Hooper dragged you out of the car. Can they trace the gun?'

'I don't think so,' he said worriedly. 'I don't have a licence.'

'No talking,' roared the sheriff. 'All right men, you four stay here. The rest of you get back to headquarters. And take these three with you.'

'Oh brother,' moaned Thompson. 'Am I ever going to get to bed?'

14

At eight o'clock that evening I leaned on a doorbell. The magnolia was very strong tonight. Ling looked at me, then with quick recognition, swung the door wide.

'Oh yes, Mr. Preston. Very fine visitor. Most welcome this house. Please to come this way.'

I please went that way. Betsy Lishman was coming down the stairs, swinging a Leica by a strap as if it were a two dollar purse.

'I'm a camera bug,' she greeted.

'Well don't let anybody see the way you treat the equipment,' I warned. 'They could think you were an anti-camera bug.'

She grinned, and it was warming.

'I have a great name for keeping my nose out of other people's business, Mr. Preston. Ask anybody.'

'I will.'

'So I'm not asking you what that

terrible business was all about last night.'

'Good. I notice you're still speaking to me.'

She nodded, and her eyes were serious now.

'I know it had something to do with Dad. He was in trouble of some kind, bad trouble. And you helped him.'

I looked innocent.

'What makes you think so?'

'You were both there last night, when those awful things happened. That maniac — Ventura? — he might have killed you both. Yet you told the police my father was a stranger to you.'

'How do you know that?'

For a moment I was afraid Lishman had been talking too much. She pursed her lips.

'If it's supposed to be a secret, you ought to tell the newspapers. It's in every evening edition, and I've read 'em all. They all say the same, my father just happened along.'

'Then they must be right,' I suggested.

'They also say you and your friend never saw my father before,' she countered. 'Are they right about that, too?'

Ling shuffled his feet and coughed.

'Just coming,' I told him. 'Betsy, maybe you should talk to your father.'

'I tried. He told me the subject was closed. He also told me we were very lucky to know someone like you.'

I stared at the floor as though I didn't know what to say. I didn't. Suddenly she leaned forward and kissed me softly on the cheek. I felt about eighty years old.

'Bless you Mr. Preston, whatever it was.'

And she was gone. I looked at Ling. He was grinning like a cat and positively bouncing up and down on his feet.

'Most welcome this house,' he beamed.

Then he swept me along to the room where I'd seen Lishman on my last visit.

'Mister Preston,' he said importantly.

'Preston, I was never so glad to see anybody.'

The boss of F.O.L. Construction came across and shook me by the hand. He pressed me into a chair, poured us both a large slug of brandy and pushed a silver cigar box towards me.

'No thanks, I'll stick to these.'

I broke the seal on a new pack of Old Favorites and pushed one between my lips.

'I'd have come earlier, but frankly I was bushed. That clown sheriff held me till almost noon. I had to get some sleep after that.'

'Of course. Naturally. They only kept me about an hour, thanks to your version of what happened.'

'That's what I was hoping. You didn't let anything slip, did you?'

He shook his head wearily.

'No. I stuck to the story. But how do you think I feel? I killed a man. I killed him, and I let someone else take the blame.'

'Yes. But you did it for her. And Ventura, he did it for her too. As for Hooper, he doesn't matter too much. I saw what he did to Arabella Bell. The only sad feature about his death is that I wasn't the cause of it. I know how you feel, and I'm not telling you to laugh it off. But it was justified. And when the first impact wears off, it won't seem so bad.'

300

Platitudes. Why do I always wind up talking to real people in platitudes? He nodded, without conviction.

'Mr. Lishman, I'm still in trouble with the police. They don't like anything about me right now, both the city force and the sheriff's office. If they can pin anything on me, they are going to do it.'

'If there's anything I can do — ' he began.

'There is. Last night I used the name of a friend of yours. I'm sorry about it, but I was really dancing in the dark. It was lawyer Delaney. What I'd like to ask you to do — '

'It's done,' he cut in. 'Delaney was on the telephone to me this morning. He guessed there had to be some connection with what he heard on the radio. I went to see him.'

'Is he sore?' I asked pointlessly.

'Let's say he was. I didn't tell him much, but then I didn't have to. The man is a friend of mine. He said he would put things right with Irving Hughes too.'

That was good news. I don't like to use harmless people, and the Hughes thing had left a bad taste. Lishman tilted his face towards the ceiling, and a large blue ring of heavy cigar smoke drifted slowly up.

'As a matter of fact, Delaney is not such a stuffed shirt as people might think. At the end of our talk, he had come around to thinking there was some humor in the situation. Because in the first place he had tried to bluff you, at my request of course. He feels you have reversed that situation with a vengeance. Tell me, is there any charge the police can bring against you?'

'Off hand, I can think of about eight. Not from the sheriff's angle though. His jurisdiction only covers what happened at the Bluffs, and I'm clean there. The city boys know a lot more about what happened before. But Rourke, that's the boss of homicide, he isn't a small minded man. He takes a look at the whole thing, and he won't bring any small charge.

'The main thing is, Ventura was the bad boy. Ventura is dead, and the people he killed are not exactly a loss to the community. Rourke could pinch me for all kinds of things, suppressing evidence, failure to co-operate with the authorities, misrepresentation, many others. He'll think about it, too. But he's known me a long time. If he finally decides I was aimed in the proper direction most of the time, he'll close the file.'

Lishman nodded.

'But if he doesn't, I want you to know you can have any legal representation you care to name.'

'Thanks, I'll appreciate that.'

'It's little enough, after all you've done for my only daughter.'

'She's a fine girl. You must be very proud of the way she's grown up. She didn't get off to a very good beginning, did she?'

He rested his elbows on the table and talked round the clenched cigar.

'You mean, having me for a father?' he said softly. 'That was her first bad luck.'

Either I was getting some kind of double talk, or events had been too much for him.

'I don't follow you,' I told him.

'Betsy is my own daughter, my natural daughter.'

He stared into my face as he said it. All he could see was blank amazement.

'But Ventura, or rather Holland, she was his girl.'

'No. Let me tell you what happened. Joe Holland was a no-good long before he actually became a criminal. His wife Molly was a wonderful girl. I'm not going into details about the way he treated her. You can use your own imagination. But he wouldn't let her go. I was doing theater work in those days, small inside construction jobs. Molly Holland was the sweetest thing you ever saw. Finally, we fell in love. Holland was always off on one of his drinking bouts. He'd be missing two or three weeks at a time, only came back when he was broke. Betsy is my daughter, Mr. Preston.'

'And what happened when he finally killed his wife?'

Lishman's face clouded over.

'He'd known about me for some time. I'd talked with him, tried to get him to give her up. He didn't want her, not really. But he was one of those people who wouldn't part with anything he thought belonged to him. Then, that night he'd been on one of his drunks. I was working after the show closed at the old Duke Theater on 42nd Street. Holland came to see me, said he'd changed his mind. When we were out in back he suddenly hit me. I wasn't ready for him, and he really laid into me. I was in hospital three weeks. He left me in the alley and went back to — to do what he did to Molly.'

I crushed out the butt in a wooden ash-tray.

'The news clipping said there was a man there when it happened.'

'Yes. That was the story Holland told. The man got away of course. But the neighbours knew about me, so the police were quite satisfied that a man existed. And I was in hospital, so I couldn't come forward.'

'Must have been a quick trial.'

'It was. Holland was clever right through the thing. He went to the police himself, and he pleaded guilty. He probably thought he'd get away with it altogether. Some men would have. But there was so much evidence of his bad character that the judge was harder on him than he'd gambled on.'

'I see. And then later, you arranged to adopt Betsy.'

'Yes. So you see, Preston, it's really all more complicated than you imagined.'

'Yes, or Holland either. About the only right idea he ever had was for a wrong reason.'

'Don't ask me to feel anything about him. You may think he needn't have died, but remember this. If he hadn't been carrying those old clippings, Hooper and the others would never have known the story. Holland made that mess, and for once in his life, he cleared up after him. All I care about is Betsy.'

There wasn't much more to be said. I stayed around a few minutes longer, then was beamed and bobbed out by Ling. As I headed for the Chev I saw a familiar small white sport car. Stella Delaney sat behind the wheel watching me. I went over.

'Is this your regular parking lot, lady?'

She treated me to one of her lopsided smiles.

'Where's your machine-gun?' she demanded.

'I have to strap it inside a sock when I'm on the highway,' I explained. 'What are you doing here?'

'Waiting for you.'

She said it quite simply, and without flapping her eyelashes at me. I could feel my tail wagging.

'I thought after you read the newspapers I wouldn't be seeing you any more.'

'I never believe newspapers.'

'What do you believe, Miss Delaney?'

'I believe my brother. He said, quote, Preston is a very remarkable guy. I believe my friend Betsy, well almost.'

'What did she say, quote?' I demanded.

'She said, quote, you were just plain wonderful, and if she wasn't all set to marry in a few weeks time, you'd have to fight her off. I'm her best friend, so she phoned and told me you were here.'

'Well, well.'

I leaned against the side of the car looking remarkable and just plain wonderful.

'Would you be getting married in a few weeks time, Miss Delaney?'

'No sir, I'm on the shelf. Just an old spinster woman.'

We grinned. She switched on the motor, and it growled into powerful life.

'I'll bet I can beat you to 1634 Rochdale Apartments,' she mocked.

'Do I bring my machine-gun?'

'Do.'

The car slid forward a couple of feet.

'Oh, and Mr. Preston — '

The blonde head turned towards me, with a lazy smile.

'Yes ma'am?'

'Don't bother to knock.'

YOU'RE BETTER OFF DEAD
NO GOLD WHEN YOU GO
MURDER IS FOR KEEPS
THIS'LL KILL YOU
NOBODY LIVES FOREVER
NOTHING PERSONAL

We do hope that you have enjoyed reading this large print book.

Did you know that all of our titles are available for purchase?

We publish a wide range of high quality large print books including:
Romances, Mysteries, Classics
General Fiction
Non Fiction and Westerns

Special interest titles available in large print are:
The Little Oxford Dictionary
Music Book, Song Book
Hymn Book, Service Book

Also available from us courtesy of Oxford University Press:
Young Readers' Dictionary
(large print edition)
Young Readers' Thesaurus
(large print edition)

For further information or a free brochure, please contact us at:
Ulverscroft Large Print Books Ltd.,
The Green, Bradgate Road, Anstey,
Leicester, LE7 7FU, England.
Tel: (00 44) **0116 236 4325**
Fax: (00 44) **0116 234 0205**

Other titles in the
Linford Mystery Library:

DEATH CALLED AT NIGHT

R. A. Bennett

Jimmy Ellis believes his parents have died in a car crash when as a young boy he is taken to live with relatives in Australia. The years pass happily, then the nightmare comes. Terrifying images flit through his mind in the dark — all through the eyes of a child, a witness to grisly events seventeen years before. He begins to delve into the past, and soon he finds himself on the trail of a double murderer — a murderer who is prepared to kill again.

DEATH IN RETREAT

George Douglas

On a day of retreat for clergy at
Overdale House, a resident guest,
Martin Pender, is foully murdered.
The primary task of the Regional
Homicide Squad is to track down the
bogus parson who joined the retreat.
Subsequent events show that serious
political motives lie behind the killing,
but the basic lead to it all is missing.
Then, three young tearaways corner
the killer in the woods, and a chess
problem, set out on a board, yields
vital evidence.

THE DEAD DON'T SCREAM

Leonard Gribble

Why had a woman screamed in Knightsbridge? Anthony Slade, the Yard's popular Commander of X2, sets out to investigate. Furthering the same end is Ken Surridge, a PR executive from a Northern consortium. Like Slade, Surridge wants to know why financier Shadwell Staines was shot and why a very scared girl appeared wearing a woollen housecoat. Before any facts can be discovered the girl takes off and Surridge gives chase, with Slade hot on his heels . . .